CW00858049

The Congregation

The Congregation

Skeletons in the Cupboard Series Book 3

A.J. Griffiths-Jones

FOR DEANY & SARAH

Author's Note

The inspiration for this book came while on holiday with a couple of good friends, as we chatted around the pool about how some people seem to carry the world on their shoulders. Thanks to Sarah Locker and Paul Dean, my co-conspirators in the development stages.

It's never easy to create fictional characters when life is so full of lively and colourful people in the flesh. I'm forever meeting friends who relate funny family secrets to me or who have an idea for a crazy saga to feature in my work, but most of the time I simply create my imaginary town and slowly mould my characters one by one. It is the fictional people themselves who tell the secrets, sometimes they know what is beginning to unfold before I do, the sign that they have taken over and the book is no longer mine.

'The Congregation' touches upon some much deeper subjects than I have written about before but that is due to the decade in which my novel is set. It was a time when people were becoming more open, more talkative and less secretive about their hang-ups. I've also chosen my key character to be a member of the clergy, someone to whom the community should be able to depend upon in their hour of need. The Church played a key role in my own childhood and evokes a myriad of memories.

Once again the amazing cover has been created in oils by my super-talented aunt, Sylvia Caswell. She just seems to be able to capture the mood of my books so well, adding mystery and intrigue to her wonderful paintings, and a fabulous back-drop for the story to unfold.

My husband, Dave, is still hanging in there, putting up with my random disappearances and moments of inspiration when I lock myself in my study and write well into the night. He never judges and always supports me, both in emotional strength and physically with cups of strong black coffee. As my book series grows, I have many people to thank in taking this journey with me. It is never easy for an author to grow their fan base, but two people in particular have been a prominent part of my success. Susie Ballinger and Peter Coombes are a wonderful couple whom I met on my travels to Gloucestershire. This pair have been the instigators of an on-line club called 'We Love A.J's Books', which allows my readers to discuss their favourite characters, share photos and generally have a good giggle. Susie & Peter, I love you to bits, even though you're both bonkers!

To everyone who has read 'The Villagers' and 'The Seasiders', I thank you for your kindness and support, and look forward to sharing many more tales of secrets, quirky characters and pots of tea with you.

Overseas readers, please note that my books contain local expressions and British English language.

Contents

Prologue

In creating the characters you now find in this fictional mining town, my mind was drawn to my youth in 1970's England, when the fashion for flared trousers and wide collars abounded and disco music was coming to the fore. It was a time of change, when motor cars and television sets were becoming more affordable for the working class, and freedom of expression was encouraged in all walks of life. Homes were being bought instead of rented and a new craze for packaged food was beginning to grip the nation.

I decided to set the scene for this particular novel in 1975, a significant time for miners in Britain, as it was the year in which they received a 35% pay rise from the Government, to align their salaries with the average wage. Spirits were running high and there was a great sense of community across the land. Accidents in the mines were becoming fewer with new safety laws being introduced, and the threat of closure was not yet imminent.

It was a year of celebration as a young Margaret Thatcher, the daughter of a greengrocer, became the first female political party leader, showing women that with determination & fight, anything could be achieved. More women were seeking careers instead of staying at home, and a new generation of animal rights activists, anti-war campaigners and freedom of speech protestors was born. However, it also proved to be a year in which the country experienced great sadness too, with I.R.A. bombings taking many innocent lives and the country being in a temporary grip of fear, especially in and around our great cities. But nothing could deter the people of the nation in their celebration of Royal birthday's, Guy Fawkes night, Halloween, and every religious event too.

In conjuring up my characters, I took a trip down memory lane, flicking through old photographs to capture the fashions and hairstyles of the era, the places that we travelled to up and down the country and also the iconic sounds that made the 1970's such a carefree and evocative time to grow up in. I remember attending weddings and christenings where the female guests wore floppy hats and the men sported platform shoes.

Up and down the country people were taking pride in their new modern homes, painting their walls in bright colours, mowing their lawns and climbing ladders to wash their windows until they sparkled in the sun. Yes, we did indeed have sunshine in those days, despite poor old England's reputation for fog and rain. We had long summers, cool nights and winters where the snow fell so deep that our fathers were obliged to build us sleds to race down hills on. Those were the days I remember.

Chapter One

The Vicar

Archie Matthews sat looking out of the train carriage. The landscape outside had changed from sunny winter skies to a thick greyish smog that settled above the hills like a dirty sheet. He wiped the steamed up window with the sleeve of his woollen coat and wished dearly that he'd brought a flask of tea for the journey. His packet of cheese and pickle sandwiches lay uneaten on the dividing table in front of him, and the gentleman passenger opposite eyed them eagerly. Archie pushed them forward with one finger.

"Help yourself," he sighed, "I shan't eat them."

The man paused for only a second before taking the cellophane wrapper off and greedily biting into the limp bread. Archie shook his head and turned his gaze back to the scenery. He could see pockets of life, small villages, fields of sheep, sprawling dairy farms, but nothing yet of the busy coal-mining town to which he was travelling. The clickety-click of the train in motion made him feel slightly nauseous and he slipped an Imperial Mint from a small bag in his coat pocket, popping it quickly into his mouth before anyone else could raise an eye. Only another half hour and he would be arriving at his destination. He didn't relish the thought at all, in fact it stirred up a sense of dread inside him, a feeling with which he was becoming strangely familiar.

As the train came to a jolting stop, Archie stooped to check that the name on the platform sign was the same as the one on the letter that he had been sent, unfortunately it was. He quickly edged his way to the luggage rack and, in one swift movement, removed his heavy suitcases from where they had lain for the past four hours. His back ached, a constant throbbing that never went away, but pride would never allow his fellow passengers to see the pain in his face.

As the carriage door was opened by a smartly dressed porter, Archie stepped down on to the concrete and looked around. The station was agreeable enough, there was a small café, functioning ticket office, a waiting room, washrooms and a left luggage office, all of the facilities that the modern day traveller could possibly need. He looked once again at the name of the town, displayed boldly on a black and white sign, stuck to the red brick of the station wall. It was then that he noticed it for the first time. Coal dust.

"Reverend Matthews?" a voice called, "I'm here to collect you."

Archie turned, instinctively touching his clerical dog-collar out of habit and wondering how long it would stay white in this black and sooty town.

A tall, thin man in a heavy overcoat and flat cap was walking towards him, grinning as though he knew some secret joke. A thick brown scarf was wound tightly under his chin, giving the appearance that his neck was twice as long as it actually was. He looked in his mid-fifties and sucked heavily on a cigarette.

"Martin Fry," he announced, "Pleased to meet you vicar."

Archie carefully put one of his suitcases down onto the platform and offered his hand, "Hello Mr. Fry."

"Oh, call me Martin, please," the other man chuckled, taking the handle of the case and lifting it, "Blimey, what have you got in here then, the kitchen sink?"

Archie opened his mouth to speak but it seemed that Mr. Fry hadn't expected an answer to his question, as he had already started walking away, his long arms causing the luggage to only just skim the ground.

"The car's over there vicar, come on."

Archie quickened his step and followed the jovial man to the car park, where several vehicles were lined up along a picket fence. He coughed as the first proper lungful of coal dust hit, causing him to pause for a few seconds. It stung his insides like nothing he had experienced before.

"Ha, you'll get used to it in no time," Martin Fry called out, as he unlocked the boot of a bright green Ford Cortina with a black vinyl roof, "Pop your case in here."

Archie did as requested and waited for his companion to unlock the passenger door. Once inside he couldn't help but notice the cleanliness of the interior. The dashboard, controls, floor mats and rear parcel shelf were all immaculate. There was a whiff of furniture polish and the vicar couldn't help but wonder if Martin Fry was as fastidious over his home as he was with his car.

"Right then, let's get you up to the vicarage," Mr. Fry smiled, "Liz has filled the pantry for you and she's fixing up some lunch as we speak."

"Liz?" Archie enquired, wondering why on earth there was someone already in his new home.

"My wife Liz," Martin explained, "My missus is your housekeeper."

"I have a housekeeper?"

"Goodness me, doesn't that Bishop of yours tell you anything?" came the response.

As the car sped through the town, Archie Matthews clung tightly to the sides of his seat. He didn't want to say anything to the driver, but he secretly feared for his life. As they came to an abrupt halt at a set of traffic lights, the tall man at his side turned to make conversation.

"So, how far did you have to come?"

It was a direct question, one which made the vicar feel uncomfortable, but he pursed his lips and searched for an answer.

"Four hours," he replied, "From the north."

Martin Fry nodded, trying to keep an eye out for the amber light as he took in Archie's solid frame.

"It's a good place to live, this," he stated, "Full of honest working-class people."

"That's very encouraging," Archie answered, looking at the townsfolk scurrying along the streets as he sat stationary at the lights, "And do the residents all attend church?"

Martin Fry shifted the gears as soon as the green light flashed, a broad grin lighting up his face.

"I should say," he laughed, "You'll have your hands full, that's for sure."

Archie didn't quite know what to say after that, so he sat back in his seat, allowing his escort to do all the talking, which he appeared very happy to do. Martin Fry was a most hospitable man, and as he steered the motor car through the busy streets, he cheerfully pointed out the main places of interest. As useful as the information was, with the doctor's surgery, library, supermarket and main square all being identified along the way, Archie was more focussed on getting to his destination, where he dearly hoped that a hot bath might be possible. He thought back with a pang of remorse to his last home, a small modern vicarage with all amenities, where he had managed to live comfortably in quiet seclusion. He hoped that his new residence would be just as obliging in the comfort stakes.

They sped past a wide entrance, where the massive shafts of a coal mine stood cold and unmoving.

"See that brow on the hill, up there?" Martin Fry was asking, rousing the vicar from his thoughts, "Well, that's where we're heading."

Archie could see the church spire already and the wide expanse of graveyard beyond. It looked eerie.

"Right," he managed to mumble, "It looks like a sizeable building."

As they neared the church, the vicar was taken aback by the grandeur of the place. It was very obviously Norman, he thought, with a tall rectangular tower and gargoyles adorning each corner of the main building. There were two entrances, he noted, as they drove past the main gates and turned down a side track to reveal a smaller one embraced by yew trees.

"Here we are," Martin Fry announced, interrupting the clergyman's train of thought, "Welcome to your new home vicar."

Archie had been so busy taking in the church and its grounds that he hadn't noticed another set of wooden gates on the opposite side of the pathway. Beyond them, as Mr. Fry manoeuvred the car onto the gravel driveway, a huge grey stone building came into view. He could see by the expression on the vicar's face that this hadn't been what he was expecting at all.

"I'll take your luggage in while you take stock of the place," he offered, leaving Archie to haul himself out of the passenger's seat and around to the bonnet of the car, where he stared in awe for quite some time. The vicarage was huge, with at least seven bedrooms, maybe more, and from the sheer amount of windows at the front of the house, Archie could see that he was going to be rattling around inside like an abandoned orphan. He looked down at his bare hands that were beginning to turn blue.

"You'll catch your death out there vicar," a woman's voice called from the front door, "Come inside."

Archie Matthews obeyed, crunching over the tiny stones under his feet and arriving at the dark panelled doorway. He kept asking himself what he was doing here, in this place, with these people.

"Lovely to meet you Reverend Matthews," the woman enthused, "I'm Elizabeth Fry."

"Hello Mrs. Fry," Archie faltered, "I wasn't aware that the Bishop had arranged, erm, help."

The woman made a snuffling sound, as if she was ready to take charge of the situation, and quickly explained what she did.

"I've been here thirty years," she began, "Cleaned, cooked and washed for the last two vicars, with no complaints. I will be here nine until four, every day, except Sundays of course. I do require alternate Saturday afternoons off to visit my sister but I'm sure that won't be a problem, will it Reverend?"

Archie shook his head and stepped inside, "No, no problem at all Mrs. Fry."

The entrance hallway was just as grand as the outside of the building. A parquet floor stretched across the whole expanse, with a long corridor leading to the left, while on the right was a wide oak staircase which disappeared upwards to the numerous rooms above. Archie sucked in his breath.

"And where do you live Mrs. Fry?"

"In the cottage just across the way," she replied, pointing to her right as she closed the heavy door, "We're not far away if you need anything."

Archie let out a sigh of relief, one that must have been visible to his new housekeeper as his shoulders dropped a couple of inches and his face brightened. It wasn't the close proximity of the couple's house that he was comforted by, but the satisfaction of knowing that he could spend his nights alone away from prying eyes. The more solitary his existence the better, Archie thought.

Mrs. Fry was leading him down the corridor, opening doors and telling him which rooms were which. There was a thud upstairs, causing the vicar to look upwards at the ceiling, but he then realised that it was only Martin taking his suitcases upstairs. At the end of the passage, the housekeeper turned left, revealing a large, bright modern kitchen, fitted with white Formica units and a wide black Aga stove. A long beech table took centre stage in the room, giving it a cosy feel. On the table were the daily newspapers and a cream flowery jug filled with rosehip twigs.

Archie took off his coat, feeling the dampness of it from the fog outside, and placed it around the back of a chair by the Aga to dry. For the first time he was in a room bright enough to properly see Mrs. Fry.

"Let me make you a pot of tea," she was saying, clattering cups and filling the kettle, "We're going to have such fun getting to know one another."

"Mmm, indeed," Archie muttered as he watched her busily fussing around, "Tea would be nice."

He could see that Elizabeth Fry was about the same age as her husband, early to mid-fifties he guessed, which was in fact close to his own age. She was only a few inches shorter than him too, a tall woman with a very shapely figure. The years had obviously been kind to the housekeeper as she bore very few lines on her face, although probable years of home baking had added inches to her waistline. She wore tight brown polyester slacks that flared slightly at the bottom and had matched them perfectly with a crocheted waistcoat, underneath which she wore a cream polo neck jumper. Archie wondered if the Fry's had any children, but it was a passing thought, he didn't want to ask and he didn't really care.

"Sugar and milk Reverend Matthews?"

He shook his head, "Just a tiny drop of milk please Mrs. Fry. Thank you."

Archie began to realise just how weary he had started to feel from his long journey, and pulled out a chair to sit down. More than anything he just wanted to be alone.

"You know, I can take care of myself for the rest of the day," he said slowly, stifling a yawn, "If you need to go home, please do Mrs. Fry."

"Would you like me to bring you a warm supper over later?" the kindly woman ventured, "We're having a rabbit stew and you're more than welcome to a bowlful."

"No, really, nothing for me."

Mrs. Fry lifted a plate from the worktop. It was covered with another plate of the same design and when she removed the top one, a platter of assorted sandwiches were revealed.

"Oh," breathed Archie, thinking back to his abandoned packet of sandwiches on the train, "You really shouldn't have gone to any trouble."

"Nonsense, that's what I'm here for vicar," smiled Elizabeth Fry, "Perhaps you'd like me to take your tea and sandwiches through to the sitting room?"

Archie nodded, too weary to argue, and too overcome with kindness to refuse. He thought back briefly to his last home, and the constant prying of his cleaning lady, who had refused to cook, cleaned only the surfaces which were clearly visible to her and had to constantly be reminded that the private papers in his study were not to become the subject of idle gossip. Mrs. Fry seemed too good to be true. Still, Archie was a man of simple needs and he doubted whether he would need his new house-keeper to do much more than keep this massive vicarage clean.

As they padded back down the hallway to the formal sitting room, with Elizabeth Fry leading the way, Archie felt like a schoolboy being taken to the headmaster's office. It had been quite a surreal day.

"I'll leave you now, if you're sure there's nothing else" whispered the housekeeper, "Get some rest."

"I'll see you tomorrow too no doubt," called her husband from the doorway, "Your cases are upstairs."

"Thank you," Archie replied, feeling a twinge in his back as he lowered himself into a chair, "Goodnight."

Archie opened his eyes several hours later. Trying to slowly adjust his eyes to the darkness, he looked around for familiar features but, of course, there were none. A faint glimmer of moonlight shone through the window, and from that he could just about make out a couple of sofas and a bookcase. Somewhere behind the chair that he reclined in was a large clock, the pendulum ticked as it swung to and fro, causing the vicar to wonder how he had slept through such a racket.

As he gathered his senses, Archie suddenly became aware of something very large and very heavy on his lap, something that he knew had definitely not been there when he had fallen asleep. He gently put a hand down to feel the cause of the pressure on his legs and immediately he did so a loud purring sound began. Without moving the hand that touched the animal, Archie reached to his left and touched upon a table lamp which he switched on, immediately bathing the room in light.

He looked down. A huge pair of green eyes stared up at him, from the body of the biggest black cat he had ever seen.

"Hello puss," Archie whispered, "What are you doing here?"

The cat yawned loudly and stretched its front paws across the vicar's knees. Obviously it had no intention of moving anytime soon. Gently lifting the animal under its warm furry stomach, Archie placed it on the floor and got up, stretching his legs vigorously to get feeling back into them. The cat eyed him curiously.

"Come on," the clergyman smiled, "Let's see if we can find us both something to eat."

Picking up the tray of cold tea and curling sandwiches from the table in front of him, Archie opened the sitting room door and shuffled out into the corridor, carefully trying not to tread on the cat as he went. The passage was in complete darkness and it took several wary steps until he managed to find a light switch, in order to make his way along to the far end where he knew he could find the kitchen. The huge feline trotted dutifully ahead, leading the way.

After depositing the cold tea in the sink, Archie carefully opened up the sandwiches to reveal slices of ham, which he fed, at intervals, to his new friend. The cat was delighted with his unexpected snack and, between bites of meat, wrapped his body around the man's legs whilst meowing softly. With the creature fed, Archie turned his attention to his own needs. Glancing at his watch, he saw that it was midnight. A cup of something warm was first on the agenda, as it was now almost eight hours since his last cup of tea. Had he really been asleep so long? Not feeling particularly refreshed despite his hours of slumber, the vicar realised that his body must have been on the point of exhaustion to have allowed him so much rest.

A large larder cupboard stood in one corner and it was to this that Archie now turned his attention. He dearly hoped that Mrs. Fry had been kind enough to fill it with provisions. Opening one of the cupboard doors, he eyed the shelves, hoping that something would get his taste buds in motion. And there it was, the very food that would sustain him until breakfast, a tin of creamy Ambrosia rice pudding.

The vicar rummaged hurriedly in a nearby drawer until he had located a can opener and, peeling back the top, reached for a spoon and dug in. Even though it was cold, the sweetness of the dessert satisfied Archie's cravings and he didn't stop eating until the can was empty. He smacked his lips together and moved to the kettle to prepare his tea, carrying the empty tin to the bin on his way. Aware of the large green eyes still upon him, Reverend Matthews looked at the huge cat, who was now sitting comfortably on a chair, and then back down at the remnants of the rice pudding.

"What?" he laughed, "Do you want some?"

The cat didn't move, but simply licked its lips in anticipation. Archie ran his forefinger around inside the can, collecting as much of the sauce as possible. He leaned over and fed the dribbling cream to the furry bundle, who lapped at it until the vicar's finger was clean.

"I think we're going to get along just fine aren't we?" he grinned.

Carrying his tea, Archie made his way along the hallway and up the winding oak staircase, methodically switching off and then switching on different lights as he went. He had no idea where he was heading, or in which of the numerous bedrooms his luggage had been put, so he slowly opened the first door that he came to on the landing at the top of the stairs. Luckily, this appeared to be the master suite, and a huge bed took up most of the wall on the far side as he entered. The furnishings were far too chintzy and floral for Archie's simple tastes but, on sitting down, he discovered that the mattress was exceptionally soft and not only was there ample wardrobe space but a very large en-suite bathroom too.

Clicking open the catches on one of his suitcases, the vicar pulled out a pair of tartan pajamas and padded into the bathroom to put them on. Once ready for bed, he moved slowly over to close the curtains. The moon was brighter now and a steady fall of snow could be seen sticking to window-pane. It had been a cold winter so far and Archie shuddered at the thought of spending his nights in this old and freezing house. He climbed into bed and pulled the covers tightly around him. There was a thud next to him, and then a nudge as the enormous black cat nuzzled up to the vicar as if to keep himself warm.

The next morning Reverend Matthews was up at dawn. Having had more than enough sleep the previous evening and night before, he was ready to explore his new surroundings and unpack his belongings. He had washed and dressed, in black polyester trousers and a grey clerical shirt with his stiff dog collar tucked through the front neckpiece. Looking in the mirror, Archie was surprised to see that he looked both refreshed and wide awake, the usual dark circles under his eyes had faded and his smooth complexion had a pink tinge.

The contents of the two suitcases were plentiful but simple. The first contained clerical clothing, a large leather bound Bible and a hymn book while the second held a few casual items of clothing, slippers, a warm dressing-gown and various personal items, such as a shaving-set, a few framed photographs and some classic novels. After setting his favourite picture on the bedside table, a photo of himself and his younger brother in their teens, Archie peeked into each of the spare bedrooms before making his way down to the kitchen for a cup of tea.

The monstrous cat had already arrived and was now eyeing up the vicar in anticipation of being fed. A cupboard near the sink revealed a few tins of cat food and, after hunting around for an old bowl, Archie scooped out half a can of meat for the waiting feline. He had a strange feeling about this cat, although a very positive one, it was as if the creature wanted to comfort and look after him.

The vicar looked out through the wide window over the kitchen sink. He could see the church tower just ahead and a wide open field to the right. In the distance stood a small stone cottage, now covered in snow and pretty against the bleak landscape. He wondered if that was where Elizabeth Fry and her family lived. A thin wisp of smoke already curled up from the cottage chimney and the tiny shape of a dog could be seen running around in the garden. It looked a very pleasing place to live.

At nine o'clock, as promised, Mrs. Fry came in through the back door, carefully taking off her snow-covered boots, and hanging up her coat and scarf. She smiled broadly and rubbed her hands.

"Morning Reverend Matthews," she chirped, "It's bitterly cold outside today, would you like me to light you a fire in the study?"

Archie thought for a moment, "I don't expect to be doing much work yet Mrs. Fry, until I get my bearings."

"Tomorrow is Saturday," the housekeeper reminded him, "So you have your first service on Sunday."

Archie was taken aback for a moment. He reached for the newspaper, still left on the table from the day before, it read Thursday 2nd January 1975. Of course, he chided himself, because of the New Year's holiday he had travelled up mid-week and now he had only a couple of days in which to prepare his sermon. Elizabeth Fry was now at the work-top twiddling with the knob on the little transistor radio, which crackled and screeched until she found a clear signal. Archie flinched visibly as the dulcet tones of the Bay City Rollers sang 'Bye Bye Baby.'

"A fire in the study would be most agreeable," he replied, "Erm, where IS the study Mrs. Fry?"

As soon as the door opened, Archie felt that he had finally found a room in which he could spend time concentrating on church matters and could also enjoy his solitude, away from other noises.

"Reverend Wilton-Hayes left a lot of his books," Elizabeth Fry was saying, waving a hand towards the floor to ceiling bookcase that was fitted into an alcove next to the fireplace, "Plenty to read."

Archie slid a heavy dark blue volume towards him, noting the title on the spine, 'The Family Physician.'

"Well, perhaps not that one," the housekeeper scoffed, "There are some nice story books there."

The vicar pushed the heavy book back and walked over to the solid oak desk which faced full-length French windows overlooking a wide expanse of lawn. A matching chair on a swivel base sat neatly tucked into the opening and on the top of the leather blotter was a letter addressed to 'Rev. Matthews.'

Mrs. Fry was a tactful woman and knew when she was no longer needed so, lighting a match to the scrumpled up newspaper, sticks and coal in the hearth, she headed for the door, stopping only briefly.

"I'll bring you some coffee shortly," she promised, "And some digestive biscuits."

Before Archie could respond, the door was closed and he found himself alone. He looked down at the crisp white envelope in his hand. The writing was spidery and scrawled, as though the author had been in a great hurry or, perhaps more likely, had scribbled the contents as an afterthought before leaving. He pulled open the top drawer of the desk and reached inside with the hope of finding a letter opener but the space was empty, leaving him no choice but to tear the seal open by hand. There lay inside just one single leaf of paper but it took him a few seconds before he could decipher the untidy strokes and get a proper understanding of the contents.

'To my successor,

I wish you well in this bleak but beautiful country town. The people are good by and large and you will find your pews brimming with eager parishioners come Sunday Service. However, be reminded that in taking on this new flock your life will be constantly challenged and behind each closed door lie dark and mysterious secrets, including this one. I have left notes for you, take care to read them and always keep the good Lord at your side. Good luck.

Sincerely Yours,

Reverend Tobias Wilton-Hayes'

Archie felt a bead of perspiration, or perhaps it was fear, trickle down his back and disappear into the waistband of his trousers. He read through the note again, checking the curling handwriting just in case he had misread or even misinterpreted the words. No, it was definitely some kind of cryptic warning.

There was a brief knock at the door and Mrs. Fry appeared with a tray of coffee and assorted biscuits.

"I'm sorry vicar," she gasped, looking at Archie's pale cheeks, "Are you still cold?"

"No, no, I'm fine thank you," he managed to blurt out, crumpling the letter into a ball and tossing it on the fire, "Here, let me take that from you."

"I'll show you how to work the heating and hot water later," Elizabeth offered, "You must have been awfully cold when you got up this morning."

"Thank you," Archie nodded, ushering her towards the door, "Now, if you don't mind I've got to get on."

"No problem, if you need anything I'll be upstairs cleaning."

"Very well," he responded sharply, "But would you mind not going into my bedroom Mrs. Fry?"

"As you please vicar," the woman answered, slowly sucking in her breath and looking at her new employer with a very puzzled expression, "If you're sure."

"Yes, I am Mrs. Fry. Very sure indeed."

As soon as the tall woman had retreated for the second time that morning, Archie turned back towards the desk and began to look through the drawers for the notes to which the strange letter had referred.

They weren't in any of the top drawers, nor the middle ones, or the bottom ones. The clergyman was mystified.

However, after deciding to pull out every single drawer completely, he was now on his hands and knees peering right inside the cavity of the desk, with the increasing heat from the fire warming the bottom of his spine quite nicely. Archie slid his right hand all the way to the back panel, using his left to balance himself, and slowly started to feel his way across the back length of the desk. After a few minutes of futile searching, he crawled backwards, resembling a human crab, and hauled himself to his knees, cursing as his back gave a loud crunch under the sudden movement.

"Damn," he shouted, "Where is it?"

There was suddenly another knock on the door and the handle turned.

"Are you alright Reverend?" a male voice enquired. The face of Martin Fry appeared, looking as cheerful as ever, despite his concern for the cursing vicar.

"Yes, yes, I'm quite alright."

Mr. Fry entered the study without being asked, and dropped a bundle of logs onto the hearth.

"I see you've found the letter then?" he sniffed.

Archie raised his eyebrows, feeling both embarrassed at having made such a disarray of the drawers, which lay all higgledy piggledy around him and curious as to how the other man knew about the letter.

"It's up here," Martin told him, carefully reaching up to one of the topmost shelves on the bookcase and taking down a black leather journal.

Archie was too flabbergasted to say anything, so instead he silently took the book from the housekeeper's husband and looked down at the untitled cover.

He flipped open the jacket and stared at the heavy inked lettering inside. There was a simple title.

'The Congregation.'

Chapter Two

Doctor and Mrs. Evans

The following day, after a long night of tossing and turning, Archie awoke to the sound of soft purring. With all the distraction of his predecessor's journal the day before, he had forgotten to ask Mrs. Fry about the strange cat that now occupied a large portion of his bed. Still, it was a comfort to have him there.

After a long hot bath, having now had instruction on how to work the heating system, Archie pulled a thick navy sweater over his clergyman's shirt and ventured downstairs with the cat running along in front. The house was dark and eerie at first light, casting shadows in the passageways, and he couldn't help wondering about the people who had filled these rooms years before. He had read a little history about the town and its mining industry, and the church was of course well documented but nothing much had been recorded about the vicarage itself. Archie intended to find out, but firstly he must take his first steps inside what was to be his new place of work and worship. And so, after a hurried slice of toast and cup of tea, the vicar fed the black feline and wrapped himself up in his heavy woollen coat and scarf.

Standing at the gate of the churchyard, with his feet covered in a light dusting of snow, Archie stood admiring the detailed craftsmanship that had created a beautiful spire, surreal images on the stained-glass windows and menacing stone gargoyles that jeered down at him from the drainage gullies above. He had always been fascinated by the expressions on their grotesque faces and even had a small collection of photographs of them that he had taken as a boy with his beloved Box Brownie.

Taking a deep breath, Reverend Matthews lifted up the stiff latch on the arched church door and stepped inside. The outer porch consisted of a wooden pew on either side, where hymn books had been neatly piled. Above the pew on the left, a wide corkboard displayed activities such as the Christmas Nativity play, a whist drive and a small poster advertising a coffee morning. They were all out of date.

On pushing open the inner door, Archie found himself inside the most beautiful church he had ever seen. The floor was made up of huge grey flagstones, undoubtedly original from a time when the Normans had been here and a wide stone font had been crafted at the end of the aisle. Archie grimaced when he thought about conducting christenings. He wasn't too fond of children although they always seemed to take a keen interest in him. The last baby who's head he had anointed had become quite irate and had urinated all over Archie's cassock. The parents had giggled about it, but the vicar had not.

Archie turned around. Huge columns flanked each side of the long walkway, which was covered in a rich burgundy carpet, stretching the full length of his walk to the altar. It was quite dim inside, and he struggled to make out the various crucifixes and family tomb inscriptions dotted around the walls. Someone had lit a single candle, so taking it carefully in his gloved hand, Reverend Matthews tilted it in order to light the other dozen or so candles that stood on a metal display. Immediately he did so, the church became bathed in light, and the full glory of its inner chambers were now visible.

"Father, bless this beautiful church, and the people who worship here," Archie whispered, "I do not deserve such a place."

His words were met with silence and, taking a hassock from the front pew, the vicar knelt in front of the altar to say the Lord's Prayer. He also prayed for his parents, the people of this town whom he was yet to meet and for a special person gone from him but remembered with deep affection.

For the next hour, Archie explored the interior nooks and crannies of the church. He climbed up the steep steps to the bell tower, ran his fingers over the collection plate and stood momentarily in the pulpit, where tomorrow he would preach his first sermon. Everything seemed surreal, was this really his new domain? The clergyman's mind raced back to when he had received an unexpected visit from the Bishop. It had been more of an order than a request, that he move away and make a fresh start, he recalled. It was true that his old congregation had dwindled in numbers over the past few years, and it was also true that Archie had become complacent towards the needs of his parish. Here, in this busy mining town, the Bishop had promised, he would find a new zest for life and hopefully find himself again.

That had been less than three weeks ago. Taking only a fortnight to pack up his belongings, Archie had caught the train to his parent's home and spent a dull Christmas being lectured by his father on the merits of being a good priest. Of course, the senior Reverend Matthews had always pushed his eldest son to become a man of the cloth, but it had taken many years of persuasion during his university days to convince Archie that he should take his religious vows. While his fellow students drank beer and drove around in their fast cars trying desperately to impress girls, Archie had spent his evenings cooped up in his room, reading and listening to Mozart. He always knew that he was different, believing that he might even be destined for great things, but with one failed parish behind him and the prospect of having to get to know his new congregation, Archie wondered what on earth it was all for. Unlike his father, Archie had never met a suitable woman whom could share his parochial duties.

He had always been hounded by the wilder girls, who looked upon his movie star looks in awe, while the more suitable young women shied away, convinced that Archie wouldn't give them the time of day.

Feeling the rumbling of his stomach, Archie looked down at his watch. He had already been here for three hours, and he hadn't even started to prepare his sermon for tomorrow yet, he must get back to the vicarage. He closed the doors and pulled the collar of his coat up around his ears for added warmth. While he had been exploring inside, a thick blanket of snow had begun to fall on the gravestones, blurring their shapes into the white landscape and making the epitaphs on each one unreadable. Archie's shoes crunched along the gravel path as he headed for the gate. A few feet away from him, along the outer wall that skirted the graveyard, three small bouquets caught his eye. Stepping sideways onto the grass, the vicar stooped down to see. The flowers were made of silk, and lay limp and wet from the driving snow. Archie shook the ice from one of them and replaced it next to the headstone, wiping the nameplate with his other hand as he did so.

"Benjamin Wheeler," Archie read to himself, "Beloved Son."

He mentally counted the years between the birth and death of the child, he was just eight when he died.

Shuffling along, with his knees now resting on the freezing ground, Archie wiped the stone fronts on the next two graves, again shaking the artificial flowers to try to restore their shape.

"Sarah Wheeler," he mumbled, "Seven years old, and Jacqueline Wheeler, six years old."

Reverend Matthews closed his eyes and said a silent prayer for the poor children whose bodies lay in the cold ground below. The poor mites hadn't even seen their teenage years.

Back at the vicarage, Archie found Mrs. Fry mopping the kitchen floor, so he carefully took off his shoes in the doorway and hung up his damp coat and scarf on the back of the door. In the background, a man and a woman discussed the heroic rescue of a child trapped in a well, on the small portable television sitting on the corner of the worktop. In the background Archie could just read the words 'Pebble Mill at One.'

"Oh, there you are!" exclaimed the housekeeper, "I'm just getting rid of Hector's mucky pawprints."

"Hector?" quizzed the vicar.

"The cat," Elizabeth explained, "Seems he's quite taken with you vicar."

Archie tried not to smile, although he was becoming quite fond of the enormous black feline too.

"He's kind of inherited with the territory," the woman continued, "On account that he won't leave."

"Ah, I see," nodded Archie, "Well, in that case, I'd better get used to him."

Mrs. Fry squeezed out the mop and wiped her hands on a tea towel.

"I've made you some soup," she smiled, "Oxtail. It'll warm you up no end."

"Thank you," Archie replied, "It's really very kind of you."

"It's my job to look after you," Elizabeth winked humorously, "Here or in your study?"

"In the study please," the vicar answered, thinking about his phobia of having to eat in front of others, "I need to prepare my sermon for tomorrow."

The housekeeper nodded and raised her eyebrows, he really was cutting it fine, she thought.

A couple of hours later with several sheets of scribbled notes filling the waste paper basket and an empty bowl at his side, Archie sat back and slid his hands behind his head. Over the past thirty years he had written hundreds of sermons but today nothing seemed to fit this cold, industrial landscape with its cheerful inhabitants and beautiful church. He thought deeply, always going back to the thick black journal that his predecessor had left behind. The vicar felt confident that its contents were going to mould his opinion of his parishioners before he'd even met them. He was only a quarter of the way through and already he was certain that he had read too much. Suddenly there was a knock on the door.

"Sorry to interrupt," Mrs. Fry whispered, edging her way in to retrieve the soup bowl, "But Doctor Evans sent a message for you."

She slipped a small pink envelope across the desk and turned to leave.

"Just a moment," Archie faltered, tearing open the seal and quickly reading the note, "Why did the Doctor send a note in this weather? Why not telephone?"

"Oh, the lines are down," the housekeeper explained, "Won't be up again for another few days."

Archie sighed impatiently, "It says here that he's expecting me for dinner at seven."

"Ooh, that's nice," Elizabeth encouraged, "Your first official engagement."

"No, I simply can't go," Archie snapped, "I'll have to send a letter back."

By the time the vicar had gathered his thoughts and written an appropriate response, declining the invitation, it was already five o'clock and Mrs. Fry had long since gone off to visit her sister.

She had left a note taped to the refrigerator, giving directions to Doctor Evans's house with a roughly sketched map underneath her cursive handwriting.

Archie looked at it closely, it seemed the surgery wasn't very far, only a fifteen minute walk, but in the heavy snow, and walking downhill, he presumed that it might take a good deal longer to arrive. He cursed profusely under his breath. The hot-blooded male in him wanted to decline the offer of dinner and curl up in front of the television but the clergyman, who almost always got his way, had settled upon accepting the invite as a way of getting to know the members of his community.

"Damn and blast it," Archie cursed, crossing himself instinctively as he vented his frustration, "There's nothing for it but to put on a clean shirt and meet these wretched people."

As he stomped upstairs to change, a pair of deep green eyes watched from the end of the hallway. Hector was mildly amused by the human who had come into his home, he didn't quite know what to make of him.

At five minutes to seven, Reverend Matthews stood waiting for the doctor to answer his front doorbell. A sign at the side of the property read 'Surgery', but the vicar had presumed that the wide glass door at the front of the house was the one indicating the entry to the residence.

"Why hello vicar," a small portly man in gold-rimmed spectacles, and only a few strands of sandy-coloured hair, greeted him, "We're glad you could come. Marjorie's made a cottage pie."

Archie did his best to look pleased and shook the doctor's open hand.

"Good evening," he said stiffly, "Very kind of you to ask me over."

Dr. Evans led his guest into a large open-plan living and dining room, with a high but wide archway creating a subtle divide. There were flowers everywhere, from the pale pink rose-patterned cushions and curtains, to the ornamental glass tulips that were displayed on the sideboard. Even the dark green carpet bore a floral design. It reminded Archie of a poorly set-out haberdashery shop.

"Scotch old boy?" Dr. Evans asked, half expecting the clergyman to decline.

Archie ran his tongue along his lips, "Yes," he replied, "Don't mind if I do."

As it turned out, Dr. Evans had lived in the town all of his life, only disappearing for a five year period to finish his medical degree. He had inherited the practice from his father where the pair had worked alongside each other until Evans senior had passed away five years before. All of this information was given willingly and in great detail, whilst Archie sipped at his scotch and allowed his eyes to glaze over. He never did understand why people liked to share everything on a first meeting, keeping nothing back to surprise or tease with later, still at least he wouldn't need to call here too often, he reflected.

There was a great clatter of dishes and pots as the two men talked, and it continued right up until eight o'clock, at which time a small bell tinkled and a petite woman in a black dress appeared.

"Hello vicar, I'm Marjorie" she grinned, "I hope you're hungry."

Archie nodded, shook Mrs. Evans' hand and then followed his host to the dining table where an elaborate array of wine, water and sherry glasses crowded a flowery pink tablecloth.

"I've made my speciality dish ," Marjorie cooed, brushing her arm against the vicar's sleeve, "Do sit down."

Archie looked down into the woman's face, which was at too close a proximity to be comfortable. Her thick red lipstick was smeared outside the borders of her natural lip-line and the heavy scent of patchouli that she wore felt thick up inside his nostrils. He looked down, not wanting to make eye contact, and noticed that her long nails were varnished silver, and heavy gold rings adorned her wrinkled fingers.

Dr. Evans shot Archie a wink across the table as they seated themselves, "Don't mind Marge old chap," he chortled, "She's been on the cooking sherry."

The doctor opened a bottle of cabernet sauvignon and treated his guest to a tale of how he and his wife had met. The clergyman tried to be attentive but distraction came in the form of more clattering from the direction of the kitchen. When the meal finally arrived, around eight-thirty, Archie was famished and feasted his eyes upon the meal before him. Runner beans, sliced carrots and cauliflower in serving dishes, and a huge ceramic pot of cottage pie in the centre of the table. His stomach rumbled.

Marjorie sat back smiling as her husband topped up the wine glasses and encouraged his guest to tuck in.

"Help yourself," he enthused, "We don't wait on ceremony here."

"Perhaps a prayer?" Archie suggested, clasping his hands together instinctively.

"Ah yes. Sorry," Dr. Evans blushed, "What was I thinking, a prayer of course."

The vicar dropped his eyes and began a prayer of thankfulness, while Marjorie Evans drank her wine.

Archie Matthews had eaten plenty of cottage pies in his time and had to conclude that, without a doubt, the one made that evening by the doctor's wife was by far the worst. Even her husband found it hard to swallow, and both men found themselves having to resort to gulping wine in between mouthfuls, simply to get the wretched stuff down their throats.

"I say dear," Dr. Evans tactfully began, "Did you forget to add some stock to the minced beef? It's a tad watery."

Marjorie twirled her crystal glass playfully and threw her head back, "Oh dear! You know I think I did."

Archie watched the doctor flinch slightly under the woman's extravagant display of forgetfulness.

"And salt dear," the little man continued, "I think you forgot to season it too."

Mrs. Evans giggled childishly and clapped her hands together, "Ha, ha, oh so I did."

And so the meal continued for a painfully slow twenty minutes, with the two men alternately drinking, making small talk about the weather, pushing food around their plates and then bravely swallowing a mouthful just to be polite. All the time Marjorie Evans appeared to be oblivious to her own disastrous cooking skills and continued to drink steadily, but she didn't take her seductive gaze off the vicar.

"Will we see you in church tomorrow?" Archie politely enquired, hoping to steer the conversation away from the topic of snow and food, "I'm looking forward to meeting my new congregation."

"Of course," Dr. Evans smiled, "I shall be right there in the front pew. Marjorie will try her best to join us, but she does find it difficult getting up early in the mornings due to her weak disposition, don't you dear?"

His wife simply smiled and drained her glass, not taking her eyes off Archie for a second.

"Do you have a special sermon lined up for your first service?" the doctor ventured.

Archie took a sharp intake of breath. He hadn't finished his sermon!

"You know it's getting rather late," he blundered, "Perhaps I should get going."

"Nonsense," Dr. Evans replied, standing to clear the plates, "We haven't had dessert yet. Besides, I've opened a particularly decent bottle of port for us to sample after dinner."

Archie really didn't know if his stomach was up to sampling more of Marjorie Evans's culinary mishaps but he didn't want to appear rude, besides port was his drink of choice and he wouldn't want his guests to think him ungrateful by leaving too soon. He'd just have to complete his sermon later.

It was just after this moment of contemplation that something very strange occurred.

Marjorie had stumbled off to the kitchen after finishing her third glass of red wine while her husband dutifully followed behind, carrying the crockery. For a minute or two the vicar was left alone to contemplate his surroundings, which if truth be told he wasn't overly impressed with. It was after this period of silence and reflection that the incident happened.

Dr. Evans had returned and was now making his way over to the teak sideboard to open another bottle of wine. As soon as the cork was popped, he returned to the table and started to refill the glasses.

"A local artist painted that," he told Archie, nodding towards a watercolour painting of the town that was mounted over the sitting room fireplace, "You can see the church in the background."

Archie instinctively turned around in his chair to where the little man was gesturing. It was a fairly simple piece of artwork and he didn't feel the desire to comment, but still he was obliged to look at it for a while.

Trying to think of something tactful to say, the vicar swung around quickly to face his host and it was within that split second that he saw the doctor putting a tiny brown packet back into his cardigan pocket.

Dr. Evans met Reverend Matthews gaze and stood speechless, his face reddening slightly.

"I have to put Marjorie's medication into her drink," he gabbled, "Otherwise she won't take it and she becomes awfully nasty."

"Nasty?" Archie repeated, "In what way?"

"Well, violent," the doctor blushed, "She smashes things and swears like a trooper."

"And the medicine?" Archie ventured, raising his eyes to meet the other man's, "What is it?"

"Just a powder," Dr. Evans told him, lowering his voice and glancing towards the kitchen door, "A kind of tonic to settle her nerves and keep her calm."

"Does she always drink so much?" the vicar asked warily, "Not that it's any of my business of course."

The smaller man winced and nodded, "Always has done I'm afraid."

They fell into a contemplative silence, each allowing the other to have time alone with their thoughts.

"Here we are," Marjorie announced joyfully, sliding bowls of something multi-coloured and wobbly across the table to the two men, "I've made trifle!"

Archie looked down at the contents disapprovingly, it certainly didn't resemble any kind of trifle that his mother had made, nor had it even been allowed to set properly.

Dr. Evans coughed and prodded the mixture with his spoon, "Oh dear, silly Marge, you didn't let the jelly set before pouring hot custard onto it."

"Oh well, it won't affect the taste," his wife giggled, reaching for her wine, "Eat it up chaps."

Archie struggled through dessert in much the same way he had forced down his main course, the only incentive being the prospect of a glass of decent port at the end of it.

As he trudged home through the snow an hour later, Archie couldn't help but wonder about the strange relationship between Dr. Evans and his wife, and also the contents of the brown packet now tucked away in the physician's cardigan pocket. The odd little man had seemed flustered at having been caught in possession of the powder and his explanation had seemed more than slightly strange. As he strode quickly upwards, with the church now in sight, the vicar bowed his head against the snowflakes that had started to fall much faster than on his walk downhill earlier that evening. It had been a very weird first dinner engagement to say the very least, and one that would certainly trouble him for many more nights to come. As the vicarage gates came into view, Archie wondered if Hector would be waiting for his return, it was comforting to think that he might not be totally alone tonight in this great sprawling house, and the presence of the huge cat was bound to increase his chances of sleep.

Next morning, with the after effects of too much wine, topped up with a heavy heady port, Reverend Matthews lay prostrate under the eiderdown until the familiar black cat climbed on top of him and peered down into the sleeping man's face. He opened one eye and realised that it was already light.

"Holy hell," he cursed, pushing the cat away and scrambling out of bed, "What time is it?"

His familiar Mickey Mouse alarm clock ticked faithfully on the bedside table. It was nine o'clock.

"Balderdash!" Archie shouted, balling his hands into fists, "Only an hour until Sunday service!"

He darted into the bathroom and splashed cold water onto his unshaven face, flinching as the icy liquid made contact with his warm skin, while his brain quickly sprang into action, calculating how much time he had to dress, drink coffee and rummage through his files for a suitable sermon.

"Epiphany," he muttered, "I must have something somewhere about Epiphany."

As the vicar dashed around, dressing, feeding Hector, making instant coffee and sifting through old notes from his previous parish, the townsfolk were already dressed in their Sunday best and heading up the hill to greet their new clergyman. There had been a great deal of discussion in the days leading up to the arrival of Reverend Matthews and the library, public houses, post office, doctor's surgery and every shop in town had been hubs of chatter, wondering if the new man of God had a wife and children, what he looked like, his age and most important of all, how he was going to fit in to this thriving community. Therefore, at quarter to ten, when Archie was finally dressed in his long black cassock, with his hair smoothed back and his face stubble removed, a large crowd of parishioners were already gathered outside the church. Every face turned to look as their new priest came rushing through the side gate, with his bible and notes in hand, and every voice gave their opinion.

"He's really handsome, like an older Tommy Steele," whispered one of the ladies to her friend.

"I don't see a wife anywhere, do you?" asked another.

"He looks a bit flustered," joked one of the men.

"Cutting it fine too," tutted a pensioner, "Reverend Wilton-Hayes was never late."

"Shhh," hushed a companion, "He'll hear you."

As Archie reached the gathering crowd, he consciously pasted a smile onto his face and reached out his hand to those who offered theirs in greeting. It had been a very long time since he had had to familiarise himself with a new flock and the sensation was over-whelming.

"Shall we step inside out of the cold?" he suggested tactfully, ushering the congregation inside and wishing that he hadn't rushed out so hastily without grabbing his coat, "It's bitter this morning."

Martin Fry was already inside, handing out hymn books to people as they entered the great church. He caught Archie's eye over the heads of the throng and winked.

"It's alright vicar," he whispered as Archie made his way past, "Me and Liz have everything set up."

Archie looked around for his housekeeper and spotted her immediately, sitting proudly on a velveteen stool, as she played the huge pipe organ with abounding concentration. It seemed that her talents were endless.

Reverend Matthews took up his position at the pulpit and looked down at his notes. He had selected quickly but carefully, entitling his sermon 'A New Beginning'. Rather apt, he thought.

Afterwards, there was a great deal of congratulations and discussion to be had, with the general hum of approval from the townsfolk for their new clergyman. Rev. Matthews had managed to keep their attention, with only one of the octogenarians falling asleep, they said, the choice of hymns had been perfect and the sermon perfectly suited the situation of a new beginning for both the congregation and their vicar. Archie was pleased and despite not feeling entirely comfortable with so many new faces to attend to, he vowed to spend adequate time preparing next Sunday's sermon and a few hours out of each day would be spent wisely, getting to know the parishioners and lending an ear to their needs. He returned to the vicarage just after midday, feeling both relieved that his first service was over and satisfied that this change was going to give him the much needed boost that he sorely needed. The vicar reflected upon some of the comments that he'd happened to overhear too. Women had whispered about his good looks, especially the younger ones and the single ladies, some as young as twenty, had looked at him in a particular way, dreamily he thought it was, or had he just imagined it? As he changed into a thick sweater and denim jeans, Archie caught sight of himself in the bedroom mirror. He saw a much younger man looking back at him than the fifty-five year old that he was, one with drive and an athletic body, someone who could have easily modelled for those hair adverts for older men that he'd seen on television. Archie stifled a laugh.

As he padded back downstairs, followed by Hector the cat, the vicar felt a familiar rumble in his stomach and realised that, in his hurry to leave that morning, he had neglected to eat breakfast. There had been several offers of Sunday lunch, by parishioners keen to welcome the new vicar into their homes, but

Archie had declined, preferring instead to eat alone. Besides, he concluded, he wasn't completely alone as it appeared that whatever he decided to eat that day, Hector would be a more than willing compadre.

Archie turned on the little transistor radio, hoping for something to distract his thoughts from the loneliness of the vast vicarage and the hundreds of miles between himself and his parents, doubtless eating their Sunday roast. The crooning of Morris Albert reached his ears, singing gently about 'Feelings'. He switched it off and walked across to the pantry where a tin of luncheon meat sat at the front of the middle shelf. He lifted it and looked at the label.

"Shall we have Spam and eggs for lunch then Hector?" Archie questioned the cat, who was now making himself comfortable on one of the kitchen chairs, "Maybe a tin of tuna for you then."

After eating, the vicar took his sermon notes back through to the study with a cup of tea. He was fastidious over keeping his paperwork in order and wanted to return them to the correct folder and begin thinking about the many Sundays of preaching and praying still to come. The black journal still lay on Archie's desk and he was immediately drawn to it.

"Let's see what Reverend Wilton-Hayes had to say about Doctor and Mrs. Evans," he muttered flicking through the pages, as the previous evening's events, and dreadful food, once again popped into his mind. His predecessor's writing was curling and difficult to read, and there were splatters of ink on the notes where the old man had obviously pressed too heavily with his fountain pen. Archie ran one finger down the margin, searching for an indication of the medical man's name. Suddenly he saw it.

'Doctor Evans is inclined to supplement his wife's alcohol with strychnine,' he read aloud, 'He assures me that it is beneficial in keeping both her mood swings and violent intentions under control & will in no way endanger her health if the dosage is carefully prepared, although the possibility of poisoning by aforementioned powder must never be completely ruled out.'

Reverend Matthews reached for his tea, it was stone cold.

Chapter Three

Rachel Graham

As the days and weeks passed, Reverend Matthews and Elizabeth Fry learned to get along quite amicably. It wasn't an easy period for either of them, but by being straight to the point and stating their expectations, both party found that they could work together without brushing the other up the wrong way too often. Archie, for his part, felt suffocated by the housekeeper's kindness and reminders as he really wasn't used to being told that it was 'lunchtime and he really should eat something', nor was he comfortable with her going upstairs to gather his dirty laundry for washing, a chore that he found far too personal. There had been a tense exchange when the vicar had finally broached his concerns, but a mutual agreement had been found whereby Archie would load his clothes and sheets into the twin tub when required, and Mrs. Fry would wash and iron them, leaving him to put them back in their rightful place on completion.

Elizabeth soon realised that this strange new clergyman had his own particular way of doing things. For one, she had been asked not to clean the master bedroom, he would do it himself the vicar had told her. Of course she did wonder if he had valuable items in his room, and didn't trust her, but as time went on she began to feel more comfortable around Reverend Matthews and accepted that he was just a very private gentleman with slightly eccentric habits. Still, she liked him. There was something very professional about the new resident and he was certainly very easy on the eye. Besides, Hector the cat liked him, so he must be a good man.

About a month after his arrival, with several church services behind him and a growing familiarity for his new congregation, Archie received a visit late one afternoon.

Mrs. Fry had already left for the day, leaving the vicar obliged to answer his own front door when the great bell rang. It was bitterly cold outside and as he stepped into the grand hallway, Archie felt a chill through his bones. On opening the heavy wooden door he was met by a very petite woman in a red hooded duffle coat. She had thick blonde hair that had a natural wave and her cheeks were flushed pink.

"Hello vicar," the woman smiled awkwardly, "I was wondering if you were free for a moment?"

Archie stiffened his back and assumed a more professional stance, "Of course, please come in."

"Mrs. Graham," the woman said timidly as she stepped inside, "Rachel Graham."

Leading his guest into the warm study, where a fire blazed in the grate, Reverend Matthews gestured to an armchair and offered the young woman some tea.

"Oh, no thank you," she whispered, "I shan't stay long."

"In that case how can I help," Archie asked, glancing at his unfinished book on the side table, "I mean, please take your time, it's lovely to meet you Mrs. Graham."

"We met at church last Sunday," Rachel reminded him, "You commented on my singing."

"Ah, of course," the vicar countered, recollecting how the woman had sung with such gusto to 'The Old Rugged Cross', "You really do have a very good voice."

Rachel Graham blushed and cleared her throat, "Reverend Matthews I'm here to make arrangements for my husband's funeral."

Archie was taken aback for a second, he hadn't expected to be in this situation so soon in his new post and it had been quite a while since he'd had to comfort a grieving widow.

"Mrs. Graham, I'm so sorry," he faltered, "Please accept my deepest condolences."

The lady inclined her head slightly and looked away, pulling a handkerchief from the sleeve of her coat.

"Perhaps we should have some tea after all," Archie smiled, "And then we can discuss the details."

Alone in his study again after a pot of tea and more sympathy than he was completely comfortable with giving out, the vicar sat down at his desk and looked at the notes that he had just scribbled in his diary. Mr. Graham's funeral had been set for ten days' time, on a Wednesday, at two o'clock in the afternoon. There was nothing unusual about the requirements, a simple service and burial, followed by refreshments at the Graham's house. However, the poor widow had been unable to give Archie enough background on her husband to create an adequate eulogy, something which he was insistent upon getting right. Of course, he understood that the poor lady would have some degree of confusion due to her grief and he had therefore arranged to visit Rachel Graham the following day to talk about her late husband's career, friends and family, in order to create a fitting tribute. The vicar hadn't asked the poor man's age, but estimated his wife to be around thirty-five, although he could never be sure with women, the way that they fixed their hair and covered their faces in make-up. He would find out tomorrow.

That night Reverend Matthews was woken by the sound of gunshots nearby. He sat bolt upright in bed, listening for which direction they had been fired. All was quiet, but he could hear the echo of the shots resounding in his ears. He looked down at Hector, who was still curled up in a ball at his side, apparently the cat had been unaffected by the noise. Archie pulled back the covers and reached for his dressing-gown, suddenly realising that he was perspiring heavily despite the chill in the room. He padded across to the window and pulled back a corner of the heavy damask curtains. The night was dark, the moon hidden from sight by heavy clouds and the only visible sign of life being a distant light from a faraway farm building. Both inside and outside the vicarage, the night was silent.

Downstairs the only sound was that of the huge clock in the sitting room, ticking away as the pendulum swung to and fro. The vicar could find no doors or windows open to account for the frosty chill in the air, so instead made his way to the kitchen to prepare some warm milk. He absentmindedly switched on the television set on the side, but was faced with the picture of a little girl and a clown telling him that service would be resumed at 6am. The clock on the wall showed three.

Taking his drink into the study, where he felt more at home, Archie looked out into the dark night, trying to accustom his eyes to the shapes of the trees and hedgerows which created a natural boundary around the vicarage garden. There were no more shots and he felt certain that the noises had been poachers out looking for rabbits. He settled at his desk, looking at the array of papers piled neatly to one side, and sipped the warm frothy liquid. Archie looked across to the other side of the huge oak desk, where his open diary lay indicating the day of Mr. Graham's funeral. He wondered if the family had a plot in the churchyard, or if there was a particular spot in which his widow might like her beloved buried. Occasions like these always tugged at the vicar's heart due to his growing disbelief in the afterlife. It wasn't that he was losing faith, not at all, but Reverend Matthews just didn't know whether he believed in a perfect heaven any more. All of his life he had waited for affirmation that life after death existed, starting with his grandfather's death many years ago, Archie had sat up night after night waiting for something. He hadn't known exactly what to expect, maybe a bright light, perhaps a ghostly apparition, or even something precious being moved around the house, but still, after all these years, his grandfather hadn't been able to communicate from the other side.

Tearing his mind away from painful memories, the vicar turned his attention to practical matters and pulled out the heavy metal cash tin in which he kept the parish funds. The Bishop had been generous in financing Archie's needs, which were hardly extravagant, but he had just realised something very important. He had been here for almost a whole month and hadn't paid his housekeeper!

'Mrs. Fry," Reverend Matthews began later that morning, feeling slightly embarrassed at his genuine oversight, "I seem to have overlooked paying you your wages."

The housekeeper looked up from ironing a shirt and shrugged, "You don't need to," she told him, "It's taken care of by the church."

Archie frowned, not quite understanding her meaning, "Does the Bishop pay you directly?"

"Not exactly," Elizabeth murmured, hanging the grey shirt on a coat-hanger, "But it's all sorted."

"So I don't need to pay you anything?" the vicar reaffirmed.

"No, nothing at all," the woman replied, turning to smile at him, "Now, what would you like for lunch?"

At two o'clock, with his insides warmed from a toasted cheese sandwich and a large mug of tea, Archie wrapped up and set off towards the town. The snow had begun to thaw and the road felt slippery under his feet, but a pair of sturdy wellington boots managed to save him from landing on his backside several times. He was amazed at how the houses had come alive over the past few days as the ice slid from their roofs and patches of grass could be seen clearly, indicating well-kept gardens and allotments. In the background, looming down on the town like some giant creature, the coal mine shafts crunched and thundered, as they pulled their quarry from the deep pits below. Men hurried about like tiny ants, black and filthy, their faces all the same.

Rachel Graham had given her address as '43 Thorpe Street' but, as Archie stood at the crossroads looking left and right, with traffic speeding past, it didn't seem to be where she had told him. He carefully stepped off the kerb and crossed over to the other side. The only thing to do was ask someone, so he opened the door of a nearby chemist shop and stepped inside.

"Thorpe Street," pondered the busty assistant taking Archie's scrap of paper in her hand, "Yes, you need to follow the road down to the bottom, by the bus station, and then turn left. It's just there."

The vicar lifted his note from her fingers and became aware that the girl was staring at him.

"Is everything alright?" he asked, quickly slipping the paper into his coat pocket.

"Ooh yes Reverend," came the answer, "I'd say. If you ever get lonely up there in the vicarage…"

Archie felt the heat rising in his face and dashed back out into the cold air. He was both flattered and ashamed that the women around here seemed to look at him so seductively. Within a minute or two he had located Mrs. Graham's address and knocked briskly at the door of a small terraced house.

"Oh, Reverend Matthews," Rachel exclaimed, opening the door wide, "Please, do come in."

The woman was wearing a fluffy pink housecoat that came down to her ankles and her thick curly hair was held back by a wide crimson band. As he stooped to cross the threshold, straight into a small living room, the clergyman looked around at the untidy piles of magazines and clothes. An open bottle of red nail polish lay overturned on the coffee table, dribbling its contents onto the glass top.

"Would you like some coffee?" Mrs. Graham asked, shuffling over to the sofa in her heeled slippers.

Archie shook his head and took a seat in an armchair close to the door. He knew this wasn't going to be easy, it never was. "Perhaps we could talk about your husband, if you're ready?"

Rachel waved her hand at him playfully and lit a cigarette, "What do you need to know?"

They talked for ten minutes, with the vicar asking general questions about Mr. Graham's job and hobbies, and his widow answering very vaguely, sometimes even changing her mind about what her husband did and didn't like. Suddenly she cocked her head to one side and jumped up.

"Did you hear that?" she quizzed, "I think Abigail wants something."

"I'm sorry," Archie admitted, "But I didn't hear anything."

His response fell on deaf ears, as Rachel was already on her feet and heading for the stairs. He heard her talking to someone on the upper floor but could make out no voice answering back. In the several minutes it took for the widow to return, Archie sat very still, feeling as though the compact space of the house was squashing him. He let out a deep breath, just as his mother had showed him when, as a boy, he had suffered from intense claustrophobia. A step on the staircase indicated the woman's return.

"Ooh, she has me running around all day," she huffed, flopping back down onto the sofa, "What with Terry and Hester too, I'm pretty much run off my feet."

"Are those your children?" Archie questioned gently, wondering how he could help.

"No," chirped Rachel Graham, suddenly wide eyed and attentive, "Just my friends, they live here."

By three-thirty, Reverend Matthews had decided that no more could be gleaned from Rachel Graham's sketchy recollections of her husband and he put on his overcoat to leave.

"I'll come and see you again before the funeral," he promised, rubbing Mrs. Graham's shoulder gently, "I do understand how difficult things can be at this time."

"I'll be alright vicar," the woman sniffed, "I've got a house full to keep me from being miserable."

"But still," Archie insisted, "My door is always open."

As he trudged back up to the vicarage, Reverend Matthews stopped at the church to say a short prayer for Mrs. Graham and her late husband. It saddened him greatly when people were taken from their families too soon, and he sincerely hoped that Rachel would find happiness again one day. He still wasn't completely satisfied with the details that she'd given him, but Archie hoped that he could talk with some of the other parishioners, that would have fond stories to tell about Mr. Graham, on Sunday. Back at home, Archie made his excuses to Mrs. Fry and raced upstairs for a hot bath.

Soaking under a steamy mountain of bubbles, Archie felt his bones begin to relax as the hot water soothed and bathed. It had been over thirty years since back pain had first troubled him, but with the aid of thermal underwear and constant hot baths he had been able to ride out the worst days by focusing his mind on other things. Today was one of those days. There was something not quite right about Rachel Graham, Archie mused, letting the water ride over him as he dipped his head below the surface, she was far from the traditional grieving widow. As a man of the cloth, having met many husbands, wives, mothers and fathers who had lost loved ones, he had seen bereavement take many different forms. Some people handled it with dignity behind closed doors, while others wept freely, unable to contain their anguish. But somehow, Rachel Graham was different.

"Vicar?" a voice called from outside the bathroom door, disturbing his thoughts, "Doctor Evans is on the phone, he'd like you to go to dinner tonight."

Archie groaned inwardly and rubbed his face, "Thank you Mrs. Fry," he yelled, "But please tell him that I have a prior engagement this evening."

"Of course," chuckled the housekeeper, turning to leave, "Dr. Who is on the T.V. at seven."

Damn it, smiled Archie, that woman knows me too well.

Later, sitting with his feet up on the sofa watching a mad doctor with a very long stripey scarf escaping from Daleks in his Police Box time machine, Archie felt content for the first time since his arrival. He still wasn't sleeping terribly well but at least the opportunity to take an afternoon nap now and again was something conceivable. He only had to close his study door and Mrs. Fry knew not to disturb him, guessing that important church business was occupying the vicar's time. Hector the fat feline was stretched out in front of the blazing grate, his furry belly exposed to the heat and deep green eyes watching his human companion. As the television programme came to an end, Archie stood up to throw another log on the fire, subconsciously humming the theme tune to himself as he did so. The room was warm and comfortable, just as a home should be.

As the music to 'Top of the Pops' began, Reverend Matthews looked back at the screen. Young women in hot pants danced around the stage while the host tried desperately to make himself heard over a screaming live audience. Archie wondered where his own youth had gone, he didn't remember ever being excited to that extent. Picking up his empty whisky tumbler, he sauntered over to the sideboard to refill it. A couple more might ensure a good night's sleep for once, he mused, even four or five straight hours would be acceptable. As he poured the golden scotch, the vicar turned his thoughts back to the earlier dinner invitation and shook his head in disbelief. Did Doctor

Evans really expect him to go back there and endure Marjorie's cooking for a second time? Hah, as far as he was concerned, the vicarage diary was well and truly full. He did wonder about the strychnine though, an entirely different matter altogether.

Next morning, Elizabeth Fry was already polishing the sitting room by the time Archie arrived downstairs. He peered around the door sleepily and gave a low cough.

"Good morning Mrs. Fry."

"Morning vicar," she returned quickly, waving the empty whisky glass at him, "Late night was it?"

"Not at all," he snapped indignantly, "I simply had a small nip after dinner."

The housekeeper laughed, ignoring his tetchy mood, "You don't have to explain to me, we're all entitled to let our hair down in our own home."

"Quite," Archie sniffed, "I'll just go and make some coffee."

"I'll make you some scrambled eggs," the woman told him, "As a way of apology for my cheek!"

After completing his sermon for the following Sunday service, Reverend Matthews turned his attention to the upcoming funeral. He understood from Mrs. Fry that a chap from in town took care of the grave-digging and churchyard maintenance, therefore he intended to speak to him as soon as possible about the location for Mr. Graham's internment. There seemed to be plenty of available plots to the rear of the site, and he felt assured that a pleasant patch of ground near the huge weeping willow could be secured.

Rachel Graham had told the vicar that her husband had been a travelling salesman, but had been quite undecided as to what he actually sold. Of course Archie hadn't wanted to push the matter, after all the poor woman seemed to be in such a fragile state, but he did need to confirm if any friends or family would be doing a reading at the service, in order for him to set out the proceedings satisfactorily. Although it was still bitterly cold and damp outside, the clergyman resigned himself to the duty of another visit to Thorpe Street, this time via the chapel of rest to pay his respects.

Despite the size of the town, Mrs. Fry had assured Archie that there was only one Funeral Director, located at the end of the main road. It was double-fronted and bore the name of the proprietor, E.W. Morris and Sons, in gold lettering on the windows she told him.

"Why? Has somebody died?" Elizabeth called as the vicar stepped out into the passage to put on his coat and scarf, "I didn't see anything in the newspaper."

"Indeed," the reverend affirmed, "A young local man."

He could hear the housekeeper's slippers pitter pattering across the kitchen floor as she neared.

"Really? Oh my goodness! Who was it?"

'I'll explain when I get back," Archie told her, wanting to get going before he either changed his mind or got caught in another storm, "I'll be back in a couple of hours."

Elizabeth Fry passed him his woollen gloves from where she'd put them to warm on the radiator earlier.

"Goodness, you really do think of everything don't you Mrs. Fry?" he smiled, genuinely surprised.

The housekeeper grinned, showing her crooked front teeth, "Yes, well, I've had enough years of practice. There'll be some beef stew waiting for you when you get back, with dumplings of course."

Archie closed the door, a smug look already spreading across his face.

Edward Morris was probably the most cheerful funeral director that the vicar had ever had come across. The chap positively oozed friendliness and hospitality as he strode out into the reception area of his business, a curling white moustache framing his crescent-shaped mouth and rosy cheeks glowing with health. A very tight grey waistcoat threatened to pop its buttons at any second as it heaved against the strain of keeping the chubby man's huge stomach in check and Archie found it quite distracting to watch.

"Well, well, to what do we owe the pleasure Reverend Matthews?" Mr. Morris roared, his voice just as large and over-powering as his great hulking body.

"Well, I thought you might be expecting me, Mr. Morris," Archie explained, "About Mr. Graham."

"Mr. Graham?" the larger man repeated, scratching his chin, "Doesn't ring any bells vicar."

After a few minutes of amiable conversation, the two men concluded that Rachel Graham must have secured the services of another mortuary business, most definitely one in another town.

"I can't understand it really," Edward Morris admitted, "We're the only company for miles around here. Next one must be over thirty miles away."

The clergyman admitted that it was very odd, considering that Mr. Graham had been a local man, but still, if that's what his widow wished, so be it.

"I shan't keep you any longer Mr. Morris," he said politely, "You must be extremely busy."

"Yes, well," the mortician concluded, shaking Archie's hand, "There's always work to be done. See you in church on Sunday. Oh, and vicar?"

"Yes?"

"Watch out for that randy old housekeeper of yours!"

Archie stood, perplexed, not quite knowing how to answer. Surely Edward Morris was pulling his leg.

The vicar turned back from where he'd been tugging open the door and looked questioningly at the fat proprietor whose business he had mistakenly come to visit.

"You are joking of course, Mr. Morris?" he stuttered. The other man just winked.

Rachel Graham still wasn't dressed. As Archie sat across from her in the low armchair, he could see that she'd painted her toenails and curled her hair but still wore the same pink fluffy robe as on his first visit. Some of the magazines had been cleared away, but there was a still a sticky red blob on the coffee table glass where the previously spilled nail polish had leaked its contents. The vicar wanted to fetch a cloth to see if the stain could be removed. Annoyingly his eye kept being drawn to it as he spoke.

"Have you thought about someone who might like to say a few words?" he suggested, clasping his hands together, "Or perhaps your husband had a favourite poem that could be read out?"

Mrs. Graham blew smoke from her nostrils, "He didn't have many friends, and he hated poetry."

Archie coughed, he disliked smoking and in such a small room it was playing on his chest.

"What about a family member?" he continued, his eyes once again roving to the sticky red patch.

"I don't suppose they'll bother to come," the young woman told him openly, "Not very close you see."

Reverend Matthews mustered a cheerful tone and edged forward on his seat, "We can keep the service very simple then Mrs. Graham, if that's what you'd like?"

Her head tipped slowly up and down in assent, "Okay."

Feeling satisfied that at least he now had a little direction on how to conduct things, Archie asked if he might visit the chapel of rest to say a prayer over the body.

"He's not there," whispered the widow, reaching for another cigarette and avoiding the vicar's gaze.

"Then where…?"

"Upstairs," came the reply, the woman's eyes shifting upwards towards the ceiling, "He's here."

The hairs began to prickle up on Archie's neck, did these townsfolk still lay out their dead at home?

"May I go up?" he asked slowly, "I mean, if you have no objection?"

"Sure," Rachel Graham replied, flicking ash into a waste paper bin, but not attempting to move.

The vicar could see that he was going to have to go up to the bedroom by himself and rose from his seat.

"Mrs. Graham, is husband properly embalmed," he wanted to ask, but the words failed to come.

Reverend Matthews had been expecting the house to be dark upstairs, out of respect for her late husband perhaps, but instead Rachel Graham had a very bright and colourful bedroom. A purple eiderdown covered the double bed, with an assortment of cuddly toys lined up along the top of the wooden headboard. Everything seemed in order, but there was certainly no sign of Mr. Graham's body.

Edging along the landing to the next room, Archie pushed open the door and found himself facing a turquoise bathroom suite. Wind-chimes made from seashells dangled from the ceiling and a yellow rubber duck sat idly on the side of the bath. The last door along was slightly ajar and it was here that the vicar expected to meet the late gentleman in who's home he now stood. Inhaling through his nose, Archie pulled his scarf up over his cheeks and took a couple of steps forward. Nothing.

"Mrs. Graham," he called, trotting quickly back downstairs, "I thought you said…"

"Oh, I'm sorry vicar," Rachel cooed, looking genuinely confused, "He did go to the chapel of rest."

"Are you absolutely sure?" Archie insisted, "Which one?"

The woman screwed her face up, thinking deeply, "Which one? Ooh, I can't remember."

"Mrs. Graham, have you been taking anything? I mean, are you on medication?"

Rachel laughed loudly, like a child who suddenly understood a joke after being told it several times.

"No! Vicar what on earth are you suggesting?"

Archie blushed, he really had no idea how best to handle the situation, after all it wasn't every day that a young widow lost her husband's body. He contemplated phoning Dr. Evans.

"Would you like to see a doctor?" he soothed, "You seem to be in a state of confusion my dear."

The woman batted her hand at him, and reached once again for her pack of filtered cigarettes.

"I'm alright," she scorned, "Perfectly fine."

Archie wasn't so sure, after all, serious lapses of the mind, including forgetfulness could be the sign of something far more serious, he pondered. However, as much as he thought that Rachel Graham should be seen by the local physician, he dreaded the thought of coming face to face with the Evans's. Therefore, he concluded, seeing as Mrs. Graham appeared to be in no immediate danger to herself or others, he would telephone the doctor on his return to the vicarage. After that he would find the missing body.

Walking briskly back up the hill towards the church, Archie cursed as a motor car sped in the opposite direction, covering his trouser bottoms in cold, wet slush. It was turning out to be one of those days. Arriving at the vicarage gates, he briefly glanced at his watch, it was five minutes to four. Very soon Mrs. Fry would be preparing to leave.

"You'll have to reheat the stew on the stove," the housekeeper tutted, as she struggled into her thick black cardigan, "I thought you'd be back long before now."

"Mmm, so did I," Archie muttered, frowning at the transistor radio which blared out 'Stand By Your Man', "If only Tammy Wynette knew the irony of that song."

"What?" Elizabeth Fry queried, "Is everything alright vicar?"

"No, it most certainly is not Mrs. Fry," he confessed, "I've had a most peculiar day. Look I shouldn't tell you this but…"

And there it was, the whole tale came pouring out, and much to Archie's relief he felt better for it.

Mrs. Fry stood perfectly still, the only movement being a slight puckering of her lips as she listened.

"And there you have it," the vicar finished, "What a pickle I'm in. Mrs. Fry, are you alright?"

The vicarage housekeeper had suddenly put one hand on the back of a chair and bent herself over so that her head almost touched the table, a wheezing sound came from her mouth.

Archie rushed to the woman's side and helped her to sit down. Tears rolled down her cheeks.

"Let me call Dr. Evans," the vicar fussed, looking around for the telephone book.

"I'm fine," a tiny voice crackled. It was at that point that Archie realised that his housekeeper was having a fit of laughter. He stood with his hands on his hips waiting for an explanation.

"Did you meet Abigail, Terry and Hester?" Mrs. Fry eventually managed to ask. Archie shook his head.

"Oh dear," Elizabeth giggled, "She's played you for a right mug. Rachel Graham isn't married vicar. Abigail, Terry, Hester, and the handsome dead husband? They're all her invisible friends!"

Archie groaned. Why the hell hadn't he checked the black journal first?

Chapter Four

Ted Bennett

As the weeks passed, Reverend Matthews fell into a routine. He could now remember the names of about half of his congregation without being prompted by either Elizabeth or Martin Fry and he had also come to appreciate what hard-working citizens he had in his little community.

The majority of the local men were employed in the coal mines which dominated the fields on the far edge of town, nestled in a valley and shadowed by steep hillsides. Archie hadn't yet had cause to venture out of town to where the pit head bulked and groaned, but he had frequently witnessed the black-faced miners returning from their day's work, swinging their lunch boxes to and fro and chattering amongst themselves. He couldn't imagine being brave enough to do a job like that, trapped underground in the searing heat and dirt but he did have a great respect for the men who returned there day after day.

On Sundays the vicar looked upon his flock in admiration, at the sooty faces which had been scrubbed clean and the starched white shirts upon the backs of the men who had spent a week in filth and grime. Their womenfolk were dressed in their Sunday best too, and every child turned out in pristine outfits. It was a mystery to Archie how the houses of these pit workers gleamed to such high standards and he had often imagined wives, standing with their hand on hips, insisting upon the men taking off all their filthy workwear before entering through the back door.

One man who never seemed to get his hands dirty, however, was foreman and Trade Union Representative Ted Bennett. A stout, imposing man with too many teeth and too little hair, Mr. Bennett was revered by his colleagues and enjoyed the attention of those around him as he took centre stage at almost every event in town. He wasn't known for his generosity, but the vicar had found him a willing volunteer for reading psalms and could always be relied upon to pass around the collection plate until the coins were brimming to the edges. Ted had taken good measure of the new clergyman and had decided in an instance that his no-nonsense attitude would fit in well with the parishioners.

Mrs. Bennett was a small woman who liked to poke her nose into other people's business, or at least that's what Archie had been told by his housekeeper. Elizabeth Fry had been openly critical about Ted's wife when he had questioned her but it was more about her appearance than personality. There was obviously no love lost between the two women so the vicar tried his best to keep an open mind, although on several occasions after Sunday service he had noticed the foreman's wife talking very openly about goings-on in the town. Still, he knew that housewives liked to talk and as long the chatter was harmless, who was he to interfere? He never would fathom out women as long as he lived.

It was getting on towards Easter before Reverend Matthews had a chance to get to know the Bennett family better, the events starting one breezy March morning as he stood in the central aisle of the church transfixed by a stone sculpture of the Madonna.

"Beautiful, isn't she?" a deep voice called from behind him, footsteps approaching at a fast pace.

Archie turned, startled by the sudden presence of another person. Ted Bennett was striding towards him, hands deep in his trouser pockets and a heavy gold watch chain hanging down from a tweed waistcoat.

"Good Morning Mr. Bennett," the vicar replied, trying to disguise his surprise, "Yes, she is rather lovely."

The two men stood staring at the perfectly formed statue for a moment, each waiting for the other to speak.

"I need to talk to you about my mother," Ted Bennett eventually sighed, "She's had to move in with us as she's not well."

"Oh, I am sorry," Archie soothed, genuinely taken aback, "Do you need me to come and see her?"

Mr. Bennett nodded in the affirmative, "Only if you've got time Reverend, she's afraid you see."

This revelation wasn't new to Archie, in his days serving the Lord he'd met many an ill person who was neither ready nor willing to meet their maker.

"Is it terminal?" he probed, "I'm sorry, it's just....well, you know."

Ted Bennett was already nodding, "We think weeks rather than months vicar."

"I'll come this afternoon," Archie promised, putting a hand upon the other man's arm, "About three?"

"I can come and fetch you," the foreman offered, "Can't have you getting wet now can we?"

"No need..." Archie began, but wishing he'd just accepted the ride and be done with it.

"Nonsense," Ted grinned, straightening his spine, "I'll pick you up about ten to three. See you later."

And with a final wave of the hand he was gone, leaving Archie alone to contemplate his latest task, the frosty chill and stillness of the church and the beautiful stone image of the Virgin Mary.

He pulled out a deep red hassock and fell to his knees to pray.

After lunch, Reverend Matthews retreated to study. The solitude was necessary after enduring an hour of the sound of the vacuum cleaner back at the vicarage, but he also had another reason for being alone.

Sitting at the large oak desk, the vicar pulled out the black journal and flicked through until he saw 'Bennett Family' at the top of a page. Given the funeral saga for a non-existent husband he wanted to be fully prepared for what the pit foreman had in store. Sipping his hot, steamy tea, he read slowly.

'Edward Bennett is a pillar of the community, fighting tirelessly for the rights of the coalminers in this town. He has donated generously to the Church and a more upright man could not be found...'

And so the writing continued, praising the deeds of Mr. Bennett and his family. Archie scratched his stubbly chin and leaned back in the chair. It seemed as though his duty this afternoon was going to be a reasonably straightforward one, he mused, albeit a very sad one. Running his fingers along his jawline once more, the vicar stood up and headed to the bathroom for a shave. He wanted to make a good impression on the foreman's mother, after all he might not be able to comfort her for long.

At ten minutes to three, as promised, a dark car swung through the vicarage gates. Archie was ready, with his thick overcoat on and a felt trilby on his head for warmth. As he walked down the drive to the waiting motor, the vicar felt Mrs. Fry watching him from an upstairs window. He turned briskly and threw her a sharp look, at which point she feigned cleaning the window panes with a rag.

"Jump in out of the cold," Ted Bennett told him, pushing open the passenger's door, "It's freezing."

The vicar folded himself into the seat and quickly pulled the door shut.

"This is terribly kind of you," he told the driver, "I could easily have walked you know."

"Don't be daft," Ted interjected, as he turned the car around and sped off down the hill, "My Mam will be delighted to see you, even just for the chance to talk a bit."

Archie nodded, taking in the gravity of the situation, "I hope I can be of some comfort."

"She probably wants to confess her sins!" Mr. Bennett joked, "There'll be plenty of them!"

The rest of the journey was spent in quiet contemplation.

The Bennett residence was a detached white house on the east side of town, where the busy streets gave way to tree-lined avenues and a large park, complete with bandstand and children's play area. Reverend Matthews hadn't been to this side of town before and was pleasantly surprised by the contrast of the more affluent area compared to the terraced houses that he was more used to seeing. He had no idea how much a mining foreman got paid but it was obviously a considerable amount more than the other pit workers. As they pulled up outside, Mrs. Bennett appeared at the front door.

"Vicar, how kind of you to come," she enthused, patting her tight curly perm and smiling widely.

"Not at all," Archie replied, removing his hat before stepping inside, "It's my pleasure."

"Put the kettle on Doris," Ted Bennett called as he followed up the rear, "I'll show the Reverend in to see Mam."

Doris Bennett tutted as she trotted along the corridor to the kitchen, her ginger curls bouncing.

Ted Bennett beckoned Archie along the thick green carpet to another door, towards the rear of the house, where he knocked loudly before going inside.

"Mam, Reverend Matthews is here to see you."

As they stepped inside, a strong scent of Lily of the Valley wafted across the room, causing the vicar to recoil slightly. The smell reminded him of his grandmother.

"Oh, I say, I am honoured," chirped a sweet little old lady, sitting up in bed in a lavender bed jacket, "Come and sit down next to me vicar."

Archie advanced towards the wicker chair at the woman's bedside and smiled broadly.

"I'm so pleased to meet you," he said honestly, feeling relaxed in the pensioner's company, "How are you feeling today Mrs. Bennett?"

The old lady laughed, showing her few teeth and pink gums, "Oh, I can't grumble vicar."

She motioned towards her son and grinned, "You can leave us alone now Ted, I'm sure you have something that you need to do. And ask Doris to hurry up with that tea will you?"

Ted Bennett cringed as his mother dismissed him, "Actually, I've got a Union meeting to go to. I'll be back in an hour if that's ok?"

Both Archie and the old woman nodded in unison.

It turned out that old Mrs. Bennett was dying of cancer. She was aware that she only had a few months to live and was happy to live out her last weeks in her son's house, where both Ted and Wendy could pander to her every need. The poor lady was in a great deal of pain, she told the vicar, but wanted to leave the world in as dignified a state as she possibly could.

"I worry about my Ted," she said wistfully, pulling an old photograph album towards her, "He's good to his old mum but he could have had so much more out of life."

Archie gazed down at the black and white pictures that he was being shown. He could see that old Mrs. Bennett had been a glamorous young woman in her day and she positively beamed with pride as she showed off images of herself with her handsome husband and young son.

"I should say Ted's doing very well for himself," the vicar commented, "A good position at the coal mines, a lovely house and a pretty wife."

"Humff," scoffed Mrs. Bennett, raising her eyes to meet his, "You don't know the half of it."

Archie could do little but raise his eyebrows in wonder, but the moment had passed and the elderly woman was once again perusing her album of memories.

After an hour of small talk about the family photos, the townsfolk and a short tale from Ted's mother on how she'd met her husband, it was time for the vicar to leave.

"I'll take you back to the vicarage now if you like," offered Mr. Bennett, "I've got a few errands to run."

Archie pulled on his coat reached for his trilby, "Would you like me to come again next week Mrs. Bennett?"

The old lady started to chuckle but it made her cough, "I should say," she eventually managed, "You should go on 'Songs of Praise' vicar, you're more handsome than any of those clergymen on there!"

Archie blushed and put on his hat, his head tipped to hide the heat in his cheeks.

"Perhaps we could think about some songs for my funeral," old Mrs. Bennett said, suddenly becoming more serious and reflective. Archie watched her trying to pull the blanket up over her chest, her weak little arms struggling with the weight of the wool. He stepped forwards to help.

"Of course, if you feel ready," he whispered, "I'll bring a hymn book with me."

Old Mrs. Bennett fell back into her pillows and sighed, she was asleep before they'd even closed the door.

The next day was Sunday and Archie was up early after another fitful sleep. Hector the cat was waiting patiently for breakfast as he entered the kitchen and immediately scurried over to rub himself up against the vicar's legs.

"What do you want old fusspot," Archie asked moodily, "Cupboard love I suppose, once you're fed you'll be back off to bed!"

Hector purred loudly and scratched at the cupboard door, waiting for something delicious to appear.

After feeding the cat and making himself a cup of coffee, Reverend Matthews went to his study to retrieve the day's sermon which he had prepared earlier that week. The meeting with Ted Bennett's mother had inspired him to write about family bonds, faith and cherishing, as one never knew when the things we take for granted may be whisked away. As Archie pulled the sermon out of a folder, the telephone rang.

"Vicar," the familiar voice of Elizabeth Fry trilled down the line, "I'm ever so sorry but Martin's in bed with the flu, can you manage without him today?"

"Yes, yes," Archie replied, looking at his watch and running through the tasks in his mind that Mr. Fry usually helped with, "I'm ready now as a matter of fact, I can sort things out."

"Oh thank you," the housekeeper sighed, "I'll be there in half an hour to go through the music with you."

Archie slipped the phone back into its cradle, and headed towards the back door. He put on his heavy woollen coat, thick scarf and the black trilby that he worn the day before and bent down to pat Hector on the head before leaving for church. The enormous cat meowed and turned to finish his food.

Meanwhile, Archie's sermon notes lay scattered and forgotten on the desk in his study.

"Another thought-provoking sermon Reverend," Ted Bennett told Archie as he stood shaking hands with the parishioners as they left after service, "I'll tell my Mam that you said a prayer for her."

"Ah, thank you Mr. Bennett, how is she?" Archie asked, still nodding at the congregation as they left.

"Looking forward to seeing you again actually," the other man grinned, "Cheered her up no end your visit did."

Reverend Matthews touched the heavy silver cross that hung around his neck and averted his eyes. When he looked up again, Doris Bennett had appeared behind her husband.

"Oh I'm so glad I could be of some comfort, I'll pop round on Thursday if that suits?"

Ted Bennett fastened the buttons on his overcoat and nodded, "I dare say that'll be fine, although I'll be at work so can't offer to pick you up this time. Best be getting back now, come along Doris."

Archie smiled, "Of course, the walk will do me good. Goodbye, nice to see you again Mrs. Bennett."

Elizabeth Fry watched Ted and Doris Bennett disappear through the gates before coming to stand at Archie's side. He could tell that she was itching to say something by the way she was fidgeting.

"Well?" he inquired.

"Nothing!" his housekeeper retorted, before sighing and relenting, "Oh vicar, you're getting to know me too well!"

Archie pursed his lips and waited. Mrs. Fry was bursting to say something, he could feel it.

"Did you notice that everyone hurried off much quicker than usual today?" she finally asked.

"I'd just put it down to the cold weather," the vicar teased, "And the fact that it's starting to rain."

Elizabeth Fry paused to readjust a notice on the board, before saying "There's a big meeting today."

"On a Sunday?" the Reverend huffed, "It must be important."

"The miners are considering going on strike," Mrs. Fry told him, proud that she knew something that Archie didn't, "As

Union Representative it's up to Ted Bennett to strike a deal with the pit bosses."

On returning to the vicarage, alone and with the prospect of some re-heated beef stew and dumplings, Archie picked up the local newspaper and flicked through to the centre pages. He'd remembered reading something about the government plans to increase miner's wages to the national average, it wasn't going down too well with the mining companies who were seeking to delay the reform. As he scanned the article for information, a waft of thick meaty dinner distracted him and he pushed the paper to one side to read later. Of course, by the time he'd eaten and fed Hector once again, Archie was asleep on the sofa.

Bang. Bang.

Reverend Matthews sat bolt upright and looked around. The shots had been close by and this time it didn't sound like poachers. Darkness pervaded the room and he banged his leg on the coffee table as he struggled to find the switch on the side of the lamp.

"Hector," he called, genuinely concerned that the cat might be terrified at the noise outside, "Here boy."

The sitting room door swung open a fraction, just enough for the fat feline to enter. He stretched and looked up sleepily at the vicar. Hector seemed unperturbed by the gunshots.

Archie stepped over to the window and peered out into the darkness, feeling a sense of 'Déjà vu' from acting out the same ritual some weeks before. The night was still, save for a faint wind.

"Let's lock up and go to bed," he told the cat, finding a slight comfort in believing that Hector both understood and cared about him, "It's getting late."

The next morning, as he sat eating toast and marmalade at the kitchen table, Archie quizzed Elizabeth about the disturbances he'd heard the night before.

"No, can't say I noticed a thing," she admitted, "I did have the television on quite loud though, we like to watch 'Z Cars' you see. Poor Martin was still in bed but he didn't mention anything."

"How strange," the vicar pondered, more to himself than to the woman who stood at the kitchen sink.

"Oh," Mrs. Fry exclaimed, suddenly remembering something, "I threw out all those old newspapers."

Archie bowed his head and poured a fresh cup of tea, "Fine, I'll be in my study."

By Thursday, Reverend Matthews had caught up on most of the parish correspondence that he needed to attend to and had also finished his Sunday sermon. He fully intended to set it out on the kitchen table at the weekend, as it had been a struggle trying to remember what he wanted to say without his notes last Sunday. The first time in over thirty years that he'd actually had to speak from memory. As he entered the kitchen a little after eleven, Elizabeth Fry was on her hands and knees cleaning out the cupboard under the sink.

"There are enough candles under here to light up the altar for a year," she muttered hearing the vicar's footsteps behind her, "Shall I take them over to the church?"

"No need," Archie replied softly, "I like to have plenty of candles in the house."

"Very well," Elizabeth wheezed, struggling to get up, "Whatever you say."

"Are you alright?" the vicar questioned, sensing the woman's tense mood, "Have I upset you?"

"Sorry Reverend Matthews," Mrs. Fry finally managed, "It's just all this kerfuffle at the mine, folks are worried about their jobs and it's the backbone of our community."

"I see," Archie nodded, although he clearly didn't, "And when will the pit bosses make a decision?"

"Sometime today," the housekeeper imparted thoughtfully, "Ted Bennett is in talks with them now."

The clergyman's eyes lit up as he had a sudden recollection, "Of course, old Mrs. Bennett!"

It took the vicar almost half an hour to complete the long walk to the Bennett residence and he could feel his cheeks flushing from the contrast of bitter wind and the heat from his body. He stood with one hand on a concrete pillar near the driveway, wanting to catch his breath before ringing the doorbell. The house looked warm and inviting with several lights switched on and thin wisp of smoke curling up from the chimney. He'd brought a hymn book as promised and a bunch of daffodils from the vicarage garden.

Archie strode up to the door and was greeted just a few seconds later by a tired-looking Doris Bennett.

"Hello again vicar," she welcomed, holding a damp tea towel in her free hand, "Come through."

Archie took off his hat and coat in the hallway and then followed Mrs. Bennett to her mother-in-law's room. The air was heavy with the elderly woman's perfume again and he sneezed upon entering.

"Oh, I say," chirped the old lady, trying to pull herself up on the pillows, "Reverend Matthews."

"Here, let me help," offered Archie, handing the flowers to Doris, "I think we need to plump these up a bit, there we go."

Old Mrs. Bennett sighed and looked at the vicar gratefully, "Thank you, that's much better."

"I'll make some tea," coughed Doris, embarrassed that it looked as though she'd been shirking her duties to the invalid, "Could you manage some soup Mam? And how about you, Reverend?"

The vicar shook his head, "Oh no, not for me thank you, but a cup of tea, no sugar, would be lovely."

As soon as the bedroom door was closed, the old woman beckoned Archie to come closer.

"There's trouble," she whispered hoarsely, "You mark my words."

"What kind of trouble?" Archie pressed, "Do you mean between your son and his wife?"

The little pensioner guffawed and reached for his hand, "No, vicar, bigger trouble than that."

Archie raised his eyebrows and waited for more, but the moment had passed and Doris Bennett was now entering the room again with the daffodils in a crystal cut vase. She eyed the pair cautiously, as if she were aware that they had been talking about her and then went back out, leaving the door slightly ajar. The vicar turned his attention to a small hymn book that he'd quickly shoved into his pocket before leaving and opened it at a random page.

"Do you have any particular favourites?" he asked tactfully, but it was too late, the old lady was fast asleep, snoring blissfully with a thin line of saliva trickling from her lips.

After an hour of sitting patiently at Mrs. Bennett's bedside, drinking tea and watching a thick skin slowly form on the bowl of soup that had been brought in, Archie got up to leave. As he did so the front door slammed shut and he heard a man's voice calling.

"Doris, where are you?" Ted Bennett shouted, "I need you to get your father to put this in the bank."

"I'm coming," his wife yelled back, "Oh, no, not again Ted!"

As Archie rounded the corner into the main hall, he came face to face with the Union Rep, who was holding a fat brown paper package in his hand. Doris Bennett was directly behind him in the kitchen doorway. Both people looked startled to see the vicar standing between them.

"Reverend Matthews!" Ted stuttered, looking at his wife, "I had no idea, I mean I forgot you were…"

"Mr. Bennett," the vicar returned, looking from husband to wife, trying to ascertain the cause for alarm, "Your mother's fast asleep, so I'll be getting back."

The colour began to return to Ted's face as he realised the purpose of the vicar's presence in his home.

"Ah, yes, of course," he faltered, "She sleeps a lot lately."

Archie pointed towards the coat hook, "If I could just grab my things…"

Ted Bennett stepped aside to let the vicar pass, sliding the brown parcel behind his back as he did so.

"Is everything alright?" Archie asked, sensing tension in the air, "Not that I'd want to pry of course."

"Yes vicar," Ted sighed, glancing quickly at his wife, "Despite what my delusional mother might have been telling you. She's losing her marbles you know?"

Archie struggled into his coat and tipped his hat at the other man, "I'll be off now." But then as an afterthought he said, "Oh, how are things at the mine Mr. Bennett?"

"Fine," the stouter man replied proudly, "I've convinced the workers to delay their pay rise until Christmas. That way it will give the bosses more time to get things sorted properly."

Walking back through the town, Reverend Matthews carefully thought through what he'd seen and heard that afternoon. It seemed very odd indeed to him that one minute the miners were about to go on strike and the next their Union Representative had worked miracles in getting them to agree to delayed action. The festive season was nine months away, he reasoned, a lot of money could be earned in that time, it seemed madness that the coal workers would agree to such a deal. Unless of course their revered leader had convinced them, somehow, that the rewards would be worth waiting for. And what benefit would that be to Ted Bennett, the vicar considered, unless that brown paper parcel had had something to do with it. Thirty minutes later, reaching the vicarage hungry and damp, Archie stopped to look back at the church, wondering how long it would be before they buried old Mrs. Bennett.

His question was answered by a brief phone call within the week. It seemed that the old lady had simply gone to sleep a few days after Archie's visit and never woken up again. She hadn't suffered, but the pain from the cancer inside her had simply become too much and her frail little body had given up. Archie felt sad that he hadn't really had a chance to get to know old Mrs. Bennett and made up his mind to go over to the church that very afternoon to light a candle and say a special prayer.

As Reverend Matthews sat in the front pew, with his hands clasped, mumbling the Lord's Prayer, he heard the familiar click of the porch door and a set of footsteps on the stone floor behind him. He didn't turn around, most people who came to the church in the middle of the day were like him, seeking solace and peace, but as the visitor slid into the next pew behind him, Archie's senses heightened.

"She was a good lady my Mam," the gruff voice whispered, "Honest and hard-working."

Archie waited for the man to go on, his eyes fixed steadily on the stained glass window in front of him.

"Unlike me, I'm nothing but a Judas."

There was silence as the speaker swallowed hard and considered his next words.

"I'm sure that's not true," the vicar soothed, hoping that the other man would continue, "I'm sure she was very proud of you."

"The package," the voice gulped, "You saw it as clear as day."

"Yes," Archie admitted, sitting upright and leaning back against the wooden bench, "Is there something you need to tell me Mr. Bennett?"

"I took a bribe from the mine bosses," Ted sighed, immediately wishing that he could retract the confession that had just slipped through his lips.

"And?" the vicar prompted, "What will you do come Christmas when the pay increases are due?"

"I'll be long gone," came the response, "It's more than enough for us to emigrate to Australia."

Archie spread his fingers wide and closed his eyes, thinking.

"You're going to give that money back, Ted Bennett," he said firmly, "Or so help me God I'll put you in the grave side by side with your mother!"

Chapter Five

The Brownlows

A month after Mrs. Bennett's funeral, Ted had resigned as Union Representative at the mine and Archie was beginning to feel less tense about bumping into him in the street. He wasn't sure exactly what had happened with the pit bosses but Mr. Bennett had assured him that the money had been returned and pay negotiations were in place with the new leader. It certainly hadn't done any harm that a considerable donation had anonymously found its way into the church restoration fun either. The vicar had asserted his authority on the morality of the parish and intended to keep a close eye on his wayward flock.

A week before Easter a typed letter arrived at the vicarage, informing Reverend Matthews that one of the pub landlords intended to hold a 'Whist Drive and Raffle' at his establishment. It seemed that Archie's attendance was compulsory in the guise of raffle adjudicator, a role that had been familiar to him in years gone by, although he would have preferred an excuse to decline. The event was to be held on the following day, not giving the vicar much time to mentally prepare himself but little needed to be done save press his best trousers and find a suitable prize to donate. However, being a man who disliked unfamiliar territory, he decided to call in at 'The Swan' for a quick drink that very evening. Archie had of course met the landlord, Michael

Vickers, several times before at Sunday service. Although not a regular attendee, due to having various publican duties to perform before opening hours, the vicar had found him a very jolly man with an easy-going disposition.

At seven o'clock, a tall handsome figure could be seen leaving the vicarage and heading down into the bustling town. The air was chilly with strong gusts of winds biting at the vicar's coat tails and more than once he contemplated turning back. Nevertheless, a strong sense of duty and the promise of a decent pint of beer kept Archie on track and he soon arrived at the black and white tavern.

Once a seventeenth century coaching inn, 'The Swan' was traditional both inside and out. It served good quality ales and traditional food, had friendly bar staff and a landlord who couldn't do enough for the men and women who partook of his wares. The interior was spotlessly clean, despite the floor having to take the daily tread of miner's boots and each and every bottle of spirit glistened on the optics. It had everything a local pub could offer to its customers although Michael Vickers had freely admitted to Archie that, from Monday to Thursday, he struggled to fill seats in the bar. The pub kitchen was even less busy on weekdays, despite having a distinguished reputation for serving the best lamb hotpot in town, and their sticky toffee pudding could compete with that of the very best restaurants. It was baffling.

Opening the door quickly, in eagerness to get out of the cold, Archie was pleased to feel immediate warmth radiating from the open fire. Three young men, all dressed in denim jeans and wide-collared patterned shirts, turned around casually to eye up the new arrival.

"Alright vicar," Michael Vickers bellowed from the far end of the bar where he'd been studying a newspaper, "What's your tipple? Pint or a short?"

Archie removed his outer clothing and approached the bar thoughtfully, eager to quench his thirst with one of the landlord's fine cask ales.

"Good evening Mr. Vickers, a pint of your best bitter please."

The three customers at the bar stopped talking and one of them offered Archie a stool, "Sit yourself down Reverend."

Archie smiled gratefully and nodded towards the hearth, "Think I'll sit closer to the fire lads, these old bones need thawing out."

One of the men laughed loudly, "Ha, ha, that's what me dad always says."

"Now then Damian," the publican interjected, glancing at Archie's flushed face, "Sit down Reverend and I'll bring your pint over. I'm guessing you've come to chat about the Whist Drive?"

"Indeed I have," the vicar returned, searching his pockets for some coins with which to pay for his drink.

"This one's on me," Michael Vickers smiled, shaking his head, "You can spend your money tomorrow."

Archie enjoyed his evening at the pub. The young men provided a source of amusement with their frivolous banter and jukebox selections, and the landlord was most amenable, providing Archie with yet another free pint and over an hour of insightful conversation. They chatted about Harold Wilson, the pipe-smoking Prime Minister, the spate of recent I.R.A. bombings and of course the mining disputes that threatened to take hold across the nation. Michael Vickers proved a very educated and sociable companion and, apart from pauses in dialogue when he meandered off to serve his other customers, the two men impressed each other with their knowledge of current affairs. Despite having dreaded the upcoming Whist Drive on his arrival, Archie found that he was now rather looking forward to his return to 'The Swan' in anticipation. If the next welcome was half as warm, he would be alright.

Next morning, the vicar found himself refreshed and bright-eyed, having enjoyed a decent sleep after the good quality beer he'd consumed the night before. In fact, so marked was the change in his demeanour that Mrs. Fry almost checked whether she was in the right house upon entering that Friday. She did a double-take as she watched Reverend Matthews buttering toast and singing the words to David Essex's 'Hold Me Close', a tune which had been played so repeatedly on the pub jukebox that the words had become stuck in the clergyman's head. Elizabeth coughed, it seemed the best course of action.

Archie turned abruptly, waving the butter knife in one hand and his toast in the other.

"Ah, Mrs. Fry, good morning. I was just…"

The housekeeper waited, one eyebrow raised in anticipation.

"Erm, anyway," Archie quickly began, changing the subject, "Will you and your good husband be coming to the Whist Drive this evening?"

Elizabeth pursed her lips, holding back the broad grin that was threatening to escape, "Yes, I think so."

"Jolly good," the vicar continued, "Now, I really must attend to some….erm, paperwork."

"I'll bring you some coffee," Mrs. Fry called after the retreating man as he headed down the hallway, the butter knife and toast still clenched tightly between his fingers, "And some napkins."

Archie spent the morning flicking through the black journal. He wanted to see if his predecessor had made notes on Michael Vickers, it would be a shame to form a bond with the man only to find out that he was corrupt, insane or any of the other strange afflictions that seemed to possess his parishioners. However, there was nothing. It appeared that the pub landlord was, quite literally, nothing to write home about, which pleased the vicar no end.

Therefore, that evening, with a tin of finest Scottish short-bread tucked under his arm as a donation to the raffle, Archie set off once again to 'The Swan' in a very pleasant mood. Although he sincerely hoped that the event wouldn't go on for hours, he was quite looking forward to helping raise funds for a couple of local charities and also to partaking in more of Mr. Vickers' finest ale. As he arrived, Elizabeth Fry was just getting out her husband's car, a printed silk headscarf tied tightly under her chin and a slick of red lipstick on her lips. On spotting Archie she ushered Martin to hurry up and park the vehicle and rushed to link arms with her employer. The three of them stepped into the welcome heat of the pub.

It soon became apparent that some of the 'Whist' players were already getting warmed up, with some friendly matches being started on the far side of the room. Archie hadn't intended to participate in the card games but was easily persuaded by his housekeeper and, with a pint of beer in hand, he duly paid his joining fee and added his name to the growing list of ea-ger competitors. Elizabeth Fry had declined to play, as she had been given the task of selling raffle tickets, therefore the vicar squeezed himself onto a seat in the corner next to her husband.

"Cold night again vicar," Martin Fry noted, "You should have let us give you a lift."

"Well, I do like to get a reasonable amount of exercise every day," Archie explained, taking a quick sip of cold beer, "But I would be grateful on the way back if it's raining."

"Aye, no problem at all," the other man promised, reaching for his glass of lemonade.

"Do you not drink Mr. Fry?" the vicar asked, looking sharply at his own full pint.

Martin laughed, "Not when I'm driving the Reverend Matthews home from town!"

"Oh, quite," Archie frowned, "I shall only have a couple tonight myself."

During the course of the evening, Reverend Matthews spent very little money but managed to sink quite a lot of beer, thanks to the generosity of the local punters. He didn't feel drunk, but simply more at ease in his surroundings and enjoyed the company of his fellow townsfolk.

"Excuse me vicar," a well-rounded woman cooed at him, squeezing her fat thighs around the edge of the table, "I just need to pop out again."

Archie sighed. This was the third time that Eva Brownlow had needed to sidle across the seats and had subsequently disappeared for half an hour or thereabouts. He wasn't keeping track of time but it seemed to the vicar that the woman and her husband were never in the bar area together for more than thirty seconds. As soon as one showed their face, the other would disappear from sight. It really was most odd. After this instance, Archie vowed to keep an eye on the pair of them, although he knew that his currently successful run of winning card games might come to an end should he do so. Nevertheless, it was too intriguing not to follow up. Sure enough, he lost the next hand and resolved to get up to order another pint. As he did so, Eva Brownlow slipped out through the side door. Perplexed, the vicar left his money on the bar, next to his empty glass, and followed the buxom woman outside.

A long, cobbled alleyway ran the full length of the pub and it was towards the end of this that Archie glimpsed the pale blue material of Eva Brownlow's dress. Trying to keep both a reasonable distance and a close eye on his quarry, the vicar quickened his pace, thankful that his sensible rubber-soled shoes made no sound on the wet stones. At the end of the alley, he could see the woman unlatch a gate between two fence panels and ease herself inside. Archie followed and stood outside the gate listening.

"Hurry up love," a male voice urged, "I'm gasping for a pint."

"Gawd Len, how was I to know we'd be so busy tonight?" he could hear Eva retort.

"There are six bottles waiting to be filled over there," the man instructed, "And Doc Evans will be over with a few more empties in half an hour."

Archie's ears pricked up at the sound of the medical man's name.

"Alright, you go off and have a beer," Mrs. Brownlow tutted, scraping something along the floor, "But don't be too long, it's bloody freezing out here."

Sensing that the man was about to leave, Archie ducked down behind a dustbin out of sight. Sure enough footsteps approached but then stopped as the man unlatched the gate.

"Oh, Eva?" the man called in a hoarse whisper, "Chuck us that book of tickets."

There was a scuffling sound and a thud, followed by the gate opening and heavy footsteps walking away.

Reverend Matthews breathed a sigh of relief and stood up, his back crunching silently as he unfurled. There was no sign of anyone in the alley now but he could hear noises coming from beyond the gate. Prising a wooden slat upwards with his fingertip, Archie peered through.

The rear of a small white cottage stood facing the alleyway. The downstairs lights were on and the figure of Eva Brownlow could clearly be seen moving around in the largest of the two rooms. She seemed to be struggling to turn something but the vicar failed to see exactly what it was. There was a lot of cursing coming from the woman's mouth, which made her robust frame seem even more comical.

"Bloody thing," she yelled, rocking from side to side, "Bloody Len, tightening everything up!."

Archie watched, mildly amused, but none the wiser of the Brownlow's mysterious antics. It was starting to rain again, therefore he let the spy-hole fall back into place and quickly returned to the pub.

At the bar, Archie's pint stood waiting, although by now the froth had gone a bit flat and the amber liquid was room temperature. He glanced around furtively and spotted Mr. Brownlow joking with his pals.

"Glad you're back," Michael Vickers shouted over the din, as he tapped the vicar on the arm, "It's time for the raffle, folks are getting restless. Where did you disappear to?"

"Call of nature," Archie told him, thinking quickly, "I'm ready whenever you are."

The landlord grinned and handed Archie a bucket full of coloured tickets, all neatly folded into squares. From across the room Martin and Elizabeth Fry stuck their thumbs up at him.

An hour later, sitting in the back of the Fry's car, clutching a cuddly panda bear that he'd won in the draw, Reverend Matthews felt both fuzzy from beer and confused at what he'd seen that night.

"Tell me," he ventured, trying to sound casual but failing completely as the words slurred out, "Are you good friends with the Brownlows?"

The furtive glance between husband and wife was enough to tell him that they were, but the substantial quantity of beer he'd consumed caused Archie to recklessly continue his line of questioning.

"What is it they do in that kitchen of theirs?" he asked boldly, "Do you know?"

Martin Fry shot Archie a harsh look in the mirror that either said, 'Shut up vicar' or 'I'll tell you later', he wasn't quite sure which. Elizabeth continued to stare out of the window.

Archie nodded to the driver, showing that he'd understood the silent message and hugged the panda tightly. He felt too drunk to talk now anyway and couldn't wait for his head to hit the pillow.

"Here we are," announced Martin Fry pulling up outside the vicarage gates, "Do you want me to walk you to the door?"

"Don't be shilly….smilly….silly…" the vicar finally managed, hauling himself out of the back seat, "See you on Sunday."

"See you tomorrow actually," Elizabeth corrected, both amused and wearied at his drunkenness.

Reverend Matthews then spent an hour outside in the cold, driving rain, trying to find his keys.

The following day, Mrs. Fry found the vicar tucked up in bed with a hot water bottle and the cat. She tiptoed around, carrying out her duties as best she could in order to let him sleep, and then decided at noon that it was time to deliver him a dose of her home cure remedy. Knocking at the door of the master bedroom, the housekeeper slowly crept inside.

"Vicar?', she whispered, "Are you awake?"

"Mmm, oh, Mrs. Fry!" Archie mumbled, gathering the blankets around him, "I didn't hear you knock!"

"Well, I did," she insisted, "Quite loudly in fact. I've brought you some chicken broth and a hot toddy."

"Thank you," the vicar sighed, relenting slightly, "You really are very kind."

Setting the tray on his bedside table, Elizabeth moved to the window to draw back the curtains. Sunlight flooded the room and Archie squinted, raising an arm to cover his eyes.

"Eat up," his housekeeper ordered, "After that you'll be as right as rain."

The vicar pulled himself upright and sniffed at the delicious aroma wafting up from the porcelain bowl.

"I say, Mrs. Fry," he commented, feeling saliva begin to fill his mouth, "This smells amazing."

"My mother's secret recipe," Elizabeth laughed, walking away from her employer, "Miracle cure."

Incredibly, the chicken broth and strange lemony drink that Archie imbibed gave him enough strength to run a hot bath and get dressed. Hector still lazed sleepily on the bed, eyeing his companion warily.

The vicar still didn't feel completely recovered but was well enough to run his eyes over the order of service for the following day. Mrs. Fry had anticipated his rise from the bed and a crackling fire blazed in the living room. Archie once again thanked his lucky stars for this incredible woman in his house.

"Ah, there you are," Elizabeth smiled, appearing suddenly with a plate in her hand, "I've made you some sandwiches for later, fish paste."

"Thank you," Archie beamed, "That really was a remarkable tonic, may I ask what was in it?"

"No you may not," she retorted playfully, "As long as it worked, that's all you need to know."

The next day, Reverend Matthews was back to his old self, which was a bit crotchety, slightly aloof and extremely professional. His notes were in order and some cheerful hymns had been selected in a bid to raise the spirits of his congregation on this cold and miserable Spring morning.

Elizabeth Fry was glad to see the vicar well rested and with a blush of colour in his cheeks, she had been genuinely concerned about his well-being the day before, especially as the man of the cloth had no wife of his own to care for his needs. As she entered the church with her husband, the housekeeper paused for a moment to watch Archie setting out the wine chalice on the altar. Such a handsome man, she thought privately, but with such personal demons inside. She longed to find out what haunted him.

"Good morning," Archie called, seeing the couple approach, "Another wet Sunday, let's hope for a good turnout. Now let's go through the hymns shall we?"

The church was full as usual, despite the harsh weather conditions and the vicar preached with gusto and pride to a very attentive congregation. Scanning the pews for anyone not paying full attention, Archie's eyes fell upon the Brownlows' sitting three rows back, their heads lolling slowly forwards in sleep. Both husband and wife were oblivious to his scornful stare and it took a sharp dig in the ribs from the people sitting next to them to raise the couple from their slumber. Ever the professional, Reverend Matthews continued his speech without faltering until it was time for Holy Communion.

As the parishioners filed up the aisle to take their wafer and wine from the vicar, Archie kept a steady eye on the sleepy Brownlows' and looked forward to giving them a knowing look as they approached. First came Eva Brownlow, her bulky frame stumbling up to the altar as though she were on auto-pilot. Archie pressed the wafer onto her tongue and offered the chalice of wine, all the time trying to catch her eye. Eva looked up, unaware that she was being observed so closely, and dark circles were clearly visible under both eyes. Reverend Matthews looked behind the large woman and saw that her husband looked just as tired, if not worse. Administering the rest of the wine quickly and without pause, he continued the service, vowing to speak to the weary couple outside should he get chance to see them alone.

As it happened, the rest of the congregation were eager to get to their waiting cars and bicycles, keen to get to their warm homes, leaving the slow-moving Brownlows' to bring up the rear. Archie held out his left hand to Eva, placing the other on her arm. He spoke in a low voice, with genuine concern.

"Is everything alright Mrs. Brownlow? You look exhausted."

Eva nodded and shrugged her rounded shoulders, "Yes vicar, I'm fine. Just a bit tired that's all."

"We both are," Len Brownlow added, putting an arm around his wife's shoulders, "Nothing that an early night won't sort out."

"I see," Archie pondered, "You work at the mine don't you Mr. Brownlow?"

"Aye, I certainly do," Len confirmed, puffing out his cheeks, "Hard graft it is too."

"Well if you ever need to talk, or…" the vicar's voice trailed off.

The Brownlows' nodded in unison and turned to leave, Eva pulling out a navy umbrella to face the rain.

Although his conversation with the Brownlows' had been brief, it played on Archie's mind for several days afterwards. He didn't like to ask Mrs. Fry any questions about his parishioners, it just didn't seem right, so once again the vicar turned to the thick black journal.

"Leonard and Evaline Brownlow," he read, an index finger following the cursive script in order to make out the lettering, "A hard-working and honest couple, faithful to each other and good parents to their children. Money troubles have plagued the family for some time lately, as they are paying for Evaline's mother to reside in an old people's home…."

Archie sat deep in thought for a long time, wondering how the lack of sleep and money worries were affecting Eva and Len. He knew that Mrs. Brownlow had a part-time job as a cleaner at the local supermarket, but he doubted whether her salary would make a lasting impact on their expenditure. Care homes were notoriously expensive, he mused, the couple must be struggling to make ends meet. Sitting in his soft leather chair, looking out through the French windows onto the immaculate vicarage lawn, Archie wondered how he could help. He didn't have sufficient means to make a donation and besides, short-term help would only ease the pressure for a while. There must be another way. Archie began to pray.

He prayed to the Lord for an answer, hoping that a sudden bolt of inspiration would give him the resolution that he desperately needed to see. Archie knew that it was too late to rectify the sadness in his own life but if he could ease the burden for the Brownlow's he would know that God was listening.

The answer hit Reverend Matthews in the middle of the night. Putting it into action however took several more days, a few trips out of town and a lot of phone calls, causing his usual fitful sleep to become even more erratic. By Good Friday the vicar was shattered but feeling very positive.

"More tea, vicar?" Mrs. Fry asked politely, as he sat reading the morning newspaper.

"Yes please," Archie replied, pushing his cup and saucer across the kitchen table and folding up his reading material, "What do you think about helping me to arrange an Easter Egg Hunt for the local children after Church on Sunday Mrs. Fry? Of course, I can give you some time off in lieu…"

"Why vicar, I think that's a wonderful idea!" the housekeeper squealed almost jumping for joy, "And I volunteer to help, I can go to Woolworth's today if you like, you know, to buy the chocolate eggs."

"Ah, I was rather thinking of the more healthy option of painted boiled eggs," he sighed, "But of course you're right Mrs. Fry, children nowadays would prefer confectionery."

Elizabeth poured tea into the china cup and studied Archie's face, something had shifted and the man's features looked softer, kinder even.

"If you don't mind me asking," she ventured, "What's brought this on?"

"Nothing in particular," he shrugged, "Just thought it would be a nice thing to do."

Mrs. Fry turned her attention to the hot cross buns she was making. Wonders would never cease, she thought.

That afternoon, Reverend Matthews set off into town to explain his plan to the Brownlow family. He dearly hoped that his intervention would be seen for the genuine concern and kindness that it was, but all too often in the past he had been on the receiving end of sharp tongues who saw his parochial duties as nothing more than meddling and nosiness. He knew that the mine was closed from mid-day due to it being a bank holiday weekend and with this in mind he hoped to catch both Eva and Len at home. Sure enough, both husband and wife were in residence, along with their two teenage boys, Gavin and Mark. It was the younger son, Mark, who answered the doorbell but, instead of inviting the vicar inside, the long-haired youth left him standing on the doorstep and disappeared into the rear of the terraced house to find his parents. Archie stood on the mat looking inside. The little terraced house was surprising hot and well lit.

"Hello Reverend," Len Brownlow called cheerfully as he made his way to the front door. A white tea towel was slung over one shoulder and furry brown slippers covered his feet, but the large man wore no shirt, just a white string vest. He was sweating profusely.

"Good afternoon," Archie smiled warmly, "I was wondering if I might have a word."

"Erm, of course," Len answered awkwardly, "It's just we're all a bit busy and…."

"Oh this won't take long," the vicar assured him, removing his hat and stepping inside, "Besides I have some very good news for you and your family."

Mr. Brownlow was stuck for words and scratched his head in wonder, "You'd better come in then."

Seated in the living room, Reverend Matthews looked around at the flock wallpaper and tan leather-look sofa. The room was neat and tidy but the pictures on the walls added nothing to enhance the décor.

"Oh I see you're a fan of Van Gogh," he noted, pointing at a framed print of the master's famous 'Sunflowers'.

"Eh?" said Len Brownlow, "Van who?"

"Never mind," huffed Archie, disappointed at the other man's ignorance of art, "Is your wife at home?"

Len Brownlow nodded and went out into the hallway to call her, leaving the vicar to admire a set of flying ceramic ducks that hung at sporadic intervals on the wall.

"Sshh," a voice whispered outside the living room door, "And don't offer him any tea."

Archie pricked up his ears. He had rather sensitive hearing and could faintly make out the conversation.

"Why didn't you tell him we were busy?" a female voice muttered, "We can't risk him staying too long."

"Alright, you pretend to be ill then," the male responded in hushed tones, "Come on…"

As the door opened, Archie turned to face the house occupants with a look of bemusement on his face, which clearly told them that he'd heard every single word.

"I don't want to put you out," he assured the couple, "But I have something to tell you."

At that very moment there was a loud bang and all three adults instinctively ran to see what had happened. Leading the way, and seeming to know exactly where the calamity had happened, Len Brownlow charged into the kitchen and let out a loud cry. Following up the rear, Archie and Eva peered inside.

The scene that greeted their eyes was one of disaster. Three-quarters of the room was full of equipment that clearly belonged in a distillery, there was a huge hole in the kitchen ceiling, clear liquid spilling out onto the floor and the most distinct smell of alcohol that Archie had ever encountered.

"A moonshine racket!" he exclaimed, looking back and forth at the Brownlow's, "So this is what you were doing on the night of the Whist Drive!"

Len looked from the hole to the vicar and then across at his two sons who were frantically trying to mop up and save some of the spirit that oozed out from the broken vat.

"It's the only way to pay for everything!" Eva yelled, seeing that they clearly needed to explain themselves, "We've got my mother's room at the care home to pay for."

Archie sighed and left the family to clear up the mess.

Later that evening, Reverend Matthews returned to the Brownlow's terraced home with an information pack and in a much more sedentary state of mind.

"And so there you have it," he finished, setting his glass of lemon squash on a side table, "I've made all the arrangements for your mother to move to the 'St. Bernadine Convalescent Home' next Monday. Her care will be financed by the nun's charity fund and it's only an extra ten minute drive away."

"And we don't have to pay a penny?" Eva asked in disbelief, "Nothing at all?"

"Nothing at all," Archie repeated, passing the bundle of documents over to her.

"So what's the catch?" Len Brownlow queried, not quite believing his ears, "There must be one."

"Nope," the vicar smiled, "Ah, well, just one. No more moonshine. Deal?"

"Deal," nodded Len, leaning forward to shake Archie's hand vigorously.

"Now perhaps 'The Swan' can earn a decent living," Archie muttered as he closed the front door.

Chapter Six

Florence Wheeler

It was the May Bank Holiday weekend and the Fry's had booked a few days away at a holiday camp, leaving Reverend Matthews to fend for himself. It didn't bother him, although the sprawling vicarage seemed to echo continuously without the noise of his housekeeper flitting about, and secretly the vicar saw it as an opportunity to eat what he liked, whenever he wanted, without anyone tutting at his choice of lunch.

Elizabeth had been prudent in sorting out church matters though, and had arranged for Doctor Evans to lend a hand with the setting out of hymn books and passing around the collection plate, while a lady called Florence Wheeler would take her place at the organ. Archie was extremely grateful to have such an efficient and thoughtful woman to help him around the place, but most of all he admired the way in which Mrs. Fry always seemed to take control without him having to worry about the little things. He thought it must be the wonderful thing that always confused him, the thing they called 'a woman's touch'.

Leaving on Friday morning, Mrs. Fry had left the larder well stocked and a note telling the vicar about the arrangements for Sunday service. However, on closer inspection, Archie thought it quite unusual that the housekeeper hadn't thought to leave him any fresh bread or cake, especially as she knew how fond he was of afternoon tea. With this in mind, he resolved to walk into town and purchase the missing items that very morning, after his customary two cups of tea, of course.

Quite unexpectedly, just as Reverend Matthews had resolved to start his trek downhill, the doorbell rang. He certainly wasn't expecting any visitors and couldn't imagine what any of his parishioners would want on a warm and sunny Friday morning. He opened the door briskly, eager to find out who was there and was greeted by a tiny woman in her forties, wearing a large floppy hat. It was Florence Wheeler.

"Good Morning Mrs. Wheeler," the vicar beamed, genuinely pleased to see his visitor, "Please come inside. Lovely morning isn't it?"

"Hello vicar," the woman smiled, stepping into the grand entrance hall, "I've brought you some bread."

Archie's ears pricked up and he looked down at the wicker basket that Mrs. Wheeler was carrying. It seemed to be filled with much more than one loaf and he wondered if she was doing multiple deliveries.

"How terribly kind," he replied, "Let's go through to the kitchen, shall we?"

Florence Wheeler nodded and followed the clergyman down the darkened corridor.

"Cup of tea?" Archie offered, thinking about the distance that his guest had just walked.

"Oh, no thank you," Florence replied timidly, setting her basket down on the table, "I have another errand to run while I'm in the area."

The pair chatted about general topics for a few minutes and then Mrs. Wheeler began to unload the products that she'd carried up the hill. There was a fresh crusty loaf, a Victoria sponge filled with cream and jam then, in the very bottom, half a dozen chocolate cookies. The other half of the large basket contained three small bunches of white roses. Archie frowned and wondered if the flowers were also meant for him.

"Beautiful bouquets," he began, "With such a delicate fragrance."

"Oh, they're for the graveyard," Mrs. Wheeler shot back, quickly pulling a white tea towel, that had covered the bread and cakes, over the top of the flowers.

"I see," the vicar said sympathetically, "Relatives?"

Florence coughed and lowered her eyes, "Yes, yes they are."

With her head bowed under the floppy hat, Archie couldn't tell if the woman in front of him was upset or not, so he thanked her profusely for the delicious goodies and looked outside at the weather.

"It's glorious out there now," he commented, "I might take a stroll to the churchyard with you."

Mrs. Wheeler lifted her chin just enough to look Reverend Matthews in the eye, sighing as she did so.

"Oh, no need vicar," she told him, "I won't be staying long, I have a long list of things to do today."

Archie understood the need to be alone at such times and followed the little lady out to the front door.

"If ever you need to…" he faltered.

Florence Wheeler straightened her shoulders and tipped her head back so that she could see the vicar properly. She was an attractive woman and wore a pale blue jacket that matched her eyes exactly.

"Thank you," she told him in a no-nonsense manner, "But I'm coping."

Archie nodded and watched the petite woman disappear through the vicarage gates, not knowing why or whom she was grieving for. It wouldn't take him very long to find out.

After returning to the kitchen and greedily devouring a large slice of the sponge cake, with yet another cup of tea, Reverend Matthews concluded that enough time had passed for

Mrs. Wheeler to have visited the grave or graves of her family and would now be on her way back home. Curiosity had got the better of him and, after pouring a saucer of milk for Hector, Archie slipped on a lightweight jacket and strolled over to the church.

It didn't take him long to spot the three small bunches of white roses, all side by side, sitting in pots on the Wheeler children's graves. His mind wandered back to a few months ago.

"Blast!" the vicar cursed, running a hand through his soft silver hair, "Why didn't I make the connection?"

He stooped down to read the inscription on one of the tombstones, a sharp twinge tugging at his lumbar region as he did so, "Benjamin Wheeler, Beloved Son."

These were the graves that he had noticed on his first proper inspection of the churchyard some time before, three young children taken from their parents far too early. There was no indication as to the cause of the three deaths, but Archie noted that the dates were all exactly the same. He presumed that some tragic accident or illness had befallen the little ones. He touched the petals on one of the white roses and felt tearful. He knew about losing someone in the prime of life, as his own wonderful brother had been called to heaven at an early age, but the grief that Florence Wheeler must be feeling would certainly be triple his own sad feelings. That poor woman, he thought.

The rest of the afternoon and well into the evening, Mrs. Wheeler played on Archie's mind. She must have thought him insensitive not to offer his condolences that morning, but how was he to know?

Sitting on the sofa, eating a fish finger sandwich with Hector at his side, the vicar flicked through the T.V. channels to find something to take his mind off things, but even the presenters on 'Blue Peter' were talking about creating a memorial garden for one of their recently departed pets. He paused for a moment, ideas rushing through his head, before being brought back down to earth by the big black cat clawing at his hand in an attempt to grab the contents of the human's sandwich.

"Hey," Archie scolded, breaking off a piece of fish, "You've had your tea, greedy boy."

Hector ignored the man's severe tone and reached up to take the offering, sniffing at it gently, before gobbling the piece in one mouthful. Archie ruffled the cat's head and gave him the rest of the fish finger.

"Arrggghhhh!!"

Archie woke in a cold sweat, with a pillow grasped tightly over his head and his face buried into the mattress. He couldn't remember all of the nightmare, but it was enough to terrify him. There had been something squashing him and the air was putrid with sweating bodies. He had struggled to find consciousness and now breathed deeply as his mind cleared from the terrors in his dream. Grabbing at the clock on his bedside table, the vicar sighed and pushed back the covers. It was 4am.

Outside in the cool breeze, Reverend Matthews stood outside the church watching the bats flying around the belfry. He could just make out the heads of the stone gargoyles in the early dawn light and vowed to read up on the history of his parish over the summer months. Crunching across the gravel path, Archie headed through the graveyard, stopping for just a second to cross himself as he approached the resting place of the Wheeler children. Archie wasn't sure whether he believed in ghosts, despite what common sense told him, but the cold wind and dark shadows were beginning to make his hair stand on end, so he moved quickly on, past the main entrance and out through the double gates onto the road.

Picking up pace as he strode downhill, Archie noticed a few lights glimmering in the houses of early risers. He presumed that it was the miners who were up, probably eating breakfast while their wives sleepily prepared lunch boxes and flasks of tea for them to take to work. He wondered what it would be like, deep underground, hot and claustrophobic with dozens of like-minded men toiling away, natural light a thing of beauty far, far above. He moved briskly, thoughts cramming his mind.

At the crossroads, the vicar had to make a decision on which way to walk. He was keen to avoid contact with too many people and decided to turn left along a row of terraced houses, which ultimately led away from town and out to the farms beyond. There was very little traffic at this time in the morning, just a few workers who either cycled or walked to the coal pit. Occasionally a door would open and a wife would say goodbye to her husband as he left their home, but for the most part the street was quiet. That was until Reverend Matthews reached the last house at the end. As he came in full view of the dark blue door with its heavy brass knocker and recently scrubbed doorstep, a familiar figure stepped out onto the pavement in front of him. It was Florence Wheeler, struggling with two heavy baskets on her arms.

"I say, Mrs. Wheeler," Archie called, rushing up to assist, "Please, let me help you."

The little woman was startled by the sight of seeing the local vicar outside her house and frowned.

"You gave me such a shock vicar," she scolded, "What are you doing creeping about at this hour?"

"I'm so sorry," Archie told her, "I just needed a stroll, to get some fresh air."

Florence pulled the baskets up high under her breasts and blinked, "Oh, an early riser are you?"

"A poor sleeper," the vicar admitted, offering a hand to take one of the loads.

Florence allowed him to take a basket and pulled the front door closed behind her.

"So, where are we off to?" Archie inquired, peering down at Mrs. Wheeler, who still looked bemused.

"This way," she sighed, turning back along the route which the vicar had not long walked, "Come on."

On reaching the crossroads, Mrs. Wheeler indicated that they would go straight over, although she seemed disinclined to speak and simply pointed to their route. Archie walked alongside silently, having to slow his usual step in order to keep up with his petite companion. He noted that Florence wasn't wearing her floppy hat today and instead had her hair covered by a navy headscarf, giving him a proper view of her profile. A pretty woman, the vicar thought, although the skin underneath her eyes was dark and puffy, showing that either she lacked sleep or cried a lot. Remembering the three headstones, Archie presumed that it was probably the latter.

"Down here," Florence Wheeler suddenly directed him, turning towards a back alley where the houses looked less affluent and a little run down.

The vicar followed obediently, shifting the heavy basket to his other arm. He wondered how Mrs. Wheeler was managing to carry such a heavy load without complaint. As a gust of wind blew down the narrow passage, Archie caught a whiff of something delicious and his stomach gave an involuntary rumble. It smelled like fruit pie warm from the oven. He looked down and realised that the wonderful aroma was indeed coming from Mrs. Wheeler's baskets. They walked on, still in silence, until the little woman stopped outside a high paneled gate and set her own basket on the ground. She lifted the cloth from the one that Archie was carrying and selected a loaf of warm bread, wrapped in brown paper, from inside.

"I'll be back in a minute," she whispered, unlatching the gate, "Wait here."

Archie did as he was asked, wondering how much his companion was charging for her bakes.

So the hour went on, with Florence Wheeler making deliveries at certain residences while the vicar waited outside. Sometimes she dropped off a simple loaf, at other times a cherry or apple pie, but it always just took but a few seconds and Archie heard no voices exchanging words.

"Have you always run a bakery?" Reverend Matthews asked casually as they made their way back through the streets with empty baskets, the sun now beginning to shine fully through the trees.

Florence eyed him cautiously, "A bakery?" she repeated.

Archie felt the heat rise in his cheeks, perhaps Mrs. Wheeler's business wasn't legitimate he considered, but merely a way of earning extra money on the side. Everyone seemed to do it these days.

"Yes, I thought...."

The small figure ignored his prying and put her free hand out to relieve Archie of the basket.

"Thank you for your help vicar," she muttered, "See you in church tomorrow."

The vicar watched Mrs. Wheeler scurry off down the street, a basket on each arm, her head bent low.

Back at the vicarage, the post had arrived and a letter from the Bishop announcing his visit the following month was enough to spark Archie into action. He wanted to ensure that both the church and the parish accounts were in tip top condition, giving his senior no room for complaint, therefore the rest of the day was spent at his desk, simultaneously planning and making lists. Florence Wheeler, for the time being, had been pushed to the back of the vicar's mind. That was until mid-afternoon, when a pot of tea became necessary to quench his thirst.

Taking the lid off the biscuit tin, expecting to find a few custard creams or bourbons, Archie was pleasantly surprised to see the freshly-baked chocolate cookies delivered that morning. He took a nibble and closed his eyes. Mrs. Wheeler really was an exceptional cook. As chips of milk chocolate melted on his tongue, Archie leaned back against the sink to savour the taste, now he could see why the little lady's baking skills were in such great demand. He calculated that they must have called at twenty houses that morning, which should generate a handsome income for a one-woman kitchen. He knew that Florence's husband worked long hours at the coal mine, on an average wage, so between them the Wheeler's must be saving a pretty packet. The only question was, with their three children six feet under, why did they do it?

The next day, Reverend Matthews arrived at the church a good hour before service. He had intended to make a thorough inspection of the building prior to the Bishop's visit, just to see if there was anything that the old man could find to tut about. Repairs were in good order, thanks to the generous weekly donations from the congregation, and numbers were good as the parishioners flooded in, so the most likely cause for complaint would be the lack of activities on offer. Archie wondered if he could rectify that by creating a local choir. As he pondered on this very matter, the porch door creaked open.

"Good morning Reverend," a tiny voice called, "Hope you don't mind me coming early."

Archie swung around from where he stood thinking on the pulpit steps and smoothed down his cassock.

"Mrs. Wheeler! Not at all my dear," he enthused, "Although service doesn't begin for a while yet."

"Yes, I know," the woman replied, setting down her handbag on a front row pew, "But it's been such a long time since I played the organ that I thought it best to have a little practice first."

"I'm sure you'll be wonderful," the vicar encouraged warmly, "But please, be my guest."

He stood up to help Florence remove her raincoat, revealing a simple black woollen dress underneath. She looked quite striking this morning, Archie thought, maybe because her hair was uncovered or perhaps the addition of some lipstick had given Mrs. Wheeler a soft glow. Still, she looked melancholy.

"Thank you," the tiny woman said, glancing briefly into Archie's eyes, "Have you made a list?"

"Oh yes," he shot back, pointing at the hymn board, "We'll start with 'All Things Bright and Beautiful.'"

Florence nodded and took a seat at the pipe organ, "Lovely, a nice happy, spring song," although the sadness in her eyes betrayed the words quite profoundly.

"I'll, erm, leave you to…" Archie began, backing away slowly, "I need to…."

Florence Wheeler ignored the vicar's feeble ramblings and took a deep breath. She then began to play.

Reverend Matthews stood breathless as he watched the tiny figure bending over the monstrous instrument, her nimble fingers dancing across the keyboard in delicate strokes, creating the most harmonious sound he had ever heard. It wasn't the hymn selection that he was expecting either, but a wonderful concerto from some bygone era. Archie stood in awe as Mrs. Wheeler played on, oblivious to her single audience member, caught up in the rhapsody which seemed to give her so much pleasure.

Later, the congregation started to arrive, chattering enthusiastically whilst taking their places in the pews. Doctor Evans seemed to enjoy his temporary position as book bearer and guardian of the collection plate, puffing out his chest with pride as he passed the silver salver amongst the parishioners. Archie had chosen 'The Good Samaritan' as his topic for the sermon, although he felt a slight pang of guilt that Mr. and Mrs. Fry weren't there to appreciate that his words were geared towards them. At the end of service however, most of the compliments were praising Florence Wheeler's musical prowess.

"Well done Florrie," Archie heard Michael Vickers telling Mrs. Wheeler as they hovered around the porch, "You did a grand job today."

Looking over heads, he could just see the little woman's face, blushing profusely.

"Really Mike," she was saying, "I'm so rusty, must be seven years since I've played."

The vicar thanked the last of his parishioners and sidled over to where the publican and organist stood.

"Mr. Vickers," he smiled, "You're quite right, Mrs. Wheeler did us proud today."

"Well, any time Elizabeth needs a break," the lady told him quietly, "I'm happy to help. Good day both."

With that, Mrs. Wheeler pulled on her coat and scurried over to where her husband was waiting at the edge of the graveyard. The two men watched them exchange a brief kiss and disappear across the grass. Both the vicar and landlord knew where the couple were heading.

"Do you know when Florrie last played the organ?" Michael Vickers asked solemnly raising his brow.

"No, actually I don't," Archie told him, "Just that it's been some years."

"It was at her children's funeral," Mr. Vickers replied in a low voice, not wanting the rest of the dwindling crowd to hear, "And such a beautiful tribute it was too."

Reverend Matthews gulped, not quite knowing what to say.

"It takes a strong woman to do that," Michael continued, "A sad day for the whole community. And yet she keeps on going, helping those in need and doing it willingly too."

'What happened?" Archie implored, genuinely feeling heart-broken for the Wheelers.

"Oh, it's a long story," the publican told him, "I'll tell you over a pint one night."

Archie spent another sleepless night tossing and turning but, instead of his usual demons, that night's terrors were full of questions on what terrible fate might have befallen Florence's three young children. He finally threw back the blankets at five o'clock and went downstairs to lay a fire in his study. The Bishop's letter still lay folded on the oak desk, its official seal turned upwards like a circle of congealed blood. Archie shivered, a strange premonition of something sinister creeping over him. Although warm sunlight was beginning to flow through the slight gap in the curtains, the vicarage felt even colder than usual, causing the vicar to head back upstairs for a sweater. As he pulled a navy cashmere over his head, Archie glanced down at the photo on his bedside table. Two happy brothers smiled back at him, one sadly taken in the prime of his life and the other now a lonely middle-aged vicar. He missed his brother dearly and today was the anniversary of his death, bringing sadness and memories flooding back.

Reverend Matthews wasn't sure how he would get through the day alone. At least if his housekeeper had been here he would have had some kind of distraction but, alone in the big house, he felt the weight of the world adding to his own personal grief. It was days like these that Archie doubted his religion.

Making pots of tea and filing away paperwork did very little to while away the time that morning and by early afternoon the vicar found himself glued to the television once again. He was aware that a myriad of characters were arguing about something on the sitcom 'Are You Being Served', but his mind couldn't focus properly on the plot so, pushing Hector from his knees, Archie switched it off. He tried retiring to the study once again, where the fire had started to dwindle, and picking up a volume of 'Barnaby Rudge' he tried his best to read. Sadly it was in vain, as the prose of Charles Dickens seemed to leave his mind just a few seconds after entering and all he could see was his brother's watery blue eyes on the day he died.

Archie wondered about the Wheeler's. How did they cope with their grief? He assumed it would be easier having someone to talk to and support you, but he neither wanted to share his story nor seek comfort. Everyone knew that the clergy were supposed to cope, relying on their God to help them through. Except in this instance, yearning to relive his childhood moments, just to see his brother alive one more time, Reverend Matthews could feel himself closing up, wanting to guard his grief from outsiders. Over the years he had built a wall, one that kept his emotions inside and his congregation at bay, in fact he hadn't even shown his heartbreak to his parents, who themselves were consumed with the death of their youngest son. But today, marking thirty two years since that fateful day when his darling brother was taken from him, right there in front of his eyes, Archie broke down and wept. He allowed the tears to flow and curled himself up in a ball on the armchair, with Hector the cat looking on in bewilderment.

The next morning Reverend Matthews awoke with a start as the back door closed with a thud. He was still in the chair and unfurled himself slowly, stretching each limb as he attempted to stand up. It was too late, Elizabeth Fry was already opening the study door, with half a dozen freshly chopped sticks in her arms.

"Oh, I'm so sorry vicar," she said with a start, "I've got some kindling for the fire."

"It's quite alright Mrs. Fry," Archie muttered, quickly smoothing a few unruly tufts of hair, "I've been up for quite some time."

Elizabeth was unconvinced. The vicar's attire was crumpled, his eyes red-rimmed and sore.

"I'll put some coffee on," she said softly, dropping the sticks onto the hearth, "Won't be long."

As the housekeeper turned to leave, Archie coughed, "Did you have a good weekend Mrs. Fry?"

"Yes, thank you vicar," she grinned, "It was just what Martin and I needed."

Getting back into a routine, with Elizabeth Fry serving meals and cups of tea at almost regimented times, was exactly the distraction from his thoughts that Archie needed. The housekeeper also had more of a spring in her step after her short holiday, lightening the mood in the vicarage and causing the vicar to realise just how much he had begun to depend and look forward to seeing her every day. The feeling was mutual, and Archie found himself being fussed around more than ever.

"Do you like Lemon Meringue Pie?" Mrs. Fry questioned later that day, "I'll make you one if you like."

"That would be very kind," Archie replied, "But I still have half the Victoria sponge cake left. I'd better eat that up first."

"Victoria sponge," Elizabeth pondered, "I didn't make you a cake."

"No, Mrs. Wheeler was kind enough to bring me some goodies," he admitted, "I thought you must know."

Mrs. Fry shook her head, "I had no idea. Although, Florrie tends to be one step ahead of the rest of the town, when it comes to people in need."

'Oh, I can hardly be classed as needy Mrs. Fry…" Archie chuckled nervously.

"You know what I mean," the housekeeper replied, shooting him a knowing look, "Florrie just cares."

That afternoon Reverend Matthews resolved to paying Florence Wheeler a visit. First he paid a short visit to her children's graves, taking note once again of their ages and date of death. He wasn't quite sure what he intended to say but at the very least he could offer a sympathetic ear.

The Wheeler's home was immaculate. The net curtains were a brilliant white, in stark contrast to the dark mahogany furniture and not a speck of dust could be seen anywhere. Florence had reluctantly invited the vicar to come in, and Archie now sat perched uncomfortably on the edge of a brown striped sofa.

"Was there something you wanted?" Mrs. Wheeler asked, her voice barely carrying across the lounge, "Only I've got cakes in the oven which will need taking out soon."

Archie cleared his throat and tried to mirror the woman's demeanour, "I just wanted to see if you're alright. Mrs. Wheeler, that's all. I understand that you must carry a lot of grief on your shoulders."

Florence shook her head, "Please, I'd rather not talk about it."

"Look," Archie sighed, I do understand, honestly I do. If ever you feel the need to share."

The tiny woman's eyes began to water but still she didn't want to unburden herself, "I'm fine."

Archie stood up to leave and touched Florence's shoulder momentarily, "I'll always be here."

She hadn't even offered a cup of tea, he thought.

Before returning to the vicarage, Archie resolved to quench his thirst with a pint of beer in The Swan. It was still early for the usual teatime punters and Michael Vickers stood polishing some sherry glasses.

"Hello vicar," the landlord greeted happily, "I knew curiosity would get the better of you."

"Sorry?" Archie replied, genuinely bewildered, "I'm not with you."

"Haven't you come to find out about the Wheeler children?" Mr. Vickers asked softly, putting down his polishing cloth and pouring the vicar a pint of best bitter.

"No," Archie admitted, "Although now that you mention it, I think I'd better hear the full story in order to help poor Florence Wheeler."

The walk back home was one of sadness and compassion.

Michael Vickers had revealed that the Wheeler children were murdered by a virtual stranger. It had happened one summer when, bored of playing on the streets, the three siblings had ventured into nearby woods to play hide and seek. It hadn't been long before they'd stumbled on the camp of a vagabond, living rough after being released from prison. Benjamin Wheeler had apparently poked fun at the straggly beard and dishevelled appearance of the man and dared his two sisters to throw stones at the stranger's makeshift tent. It wasn't known how long the taunting went on for, but it was long enough to cause the tramp to flip, chasing the youngsters through the trees and slashing them one by one with a hunting knife. After rendering the Wheeler children injured and unable to run, the ex-convict had returned to each one to finish his deadly deed. The manhunt hadn't taken long, with a local farmer finding the murderer taking refuge in his barn, but it was too late to save the wounded children. By the end of the recollection, both the publican and vicar had been tearful, with tiny globules falling into their beer. On a final note. Michael Vickers explained about Florrie's baking, which was done for pure charity, helping out those who were struggling financially or had a sick relative, and of course a lonely clergyman.

By the time Archie reached the church, he was feeling less self-absorbed about his own grief and full of admiration for the way in which the Wheeler's had coped. He crossed the graveyard to say a prayer at the children's graves and knelt down to touch their headstones.

"Father bless these tiny souls..." the vicar began, the words choking him as his thoughts raced, "They were taken from their home in early life and I pray that they are safe in heaven with you Lord."

He stopped. A couple of stones had been disturbed behind him, the footsteps slow and faint.

Archie turned around quickly, hoping to catch whoever it was sneaking up on him. It was Mrs. Wheeler.

"Sorry," she began, "Please carry on."

Archie scrambled to his feet, brushing the dirt from his knees as he did so, "Mrs. Wheeler....I..."

"I'm ready to talk," she told him meekly, "If that's alright."

Reverend Matthews nodded and rubbed both hands across his eyes, "Yes, Florrie, let's go inside."

Chapter Seven

Bill Wheatley

Bishop Honeywell was due to arrive on the eleven o'clock train. Luckily Martin Fry had managed to get a few hours free from his regular work and had agreed to drive Archie to the train station to meet his mentor. The two men now stood side by side on the platform, one smoking a cigarette and the other looking down at his freshly polished shoes.

"How long is he staying?" Martin asked casually, exhaling smoke into the vicar's face.

Archie coughed and waved a hand franticly, "Really Martin, must you? A few days I suppose."

"Nice bit of company for you then?"

"Yes, I'm sure we'll have a good deal to talk about," Archie sighed, secretly hoping that the Bishop would make this a flying visit and then be on his way to the next parish under his command.

"He's a good laugh is Wilf," Martin reflected, "Likes a drop of whisky too."

"Wilf?" the vicar repeated, raising his voice, "You're on first name terms with Bishop Honeywell?"

Mr. Fry nodded and started to explain but his words were muffled by the sound of a train approaching.

Bishop Honeywell had arrived.

A balding man of short stature and with rounded shoulders that caused him to have a slight stoop, the Bishop spoke with an upper-class accent hinting at a privileged upbringing. He shook Archie's hand warmly, his eyes twinkling with kindness and empathy.

"My dear boy," he enthused, "I do hope you're settling well, it's quite a change from your last posting."

"I'm fine," Reverend Matthews assured him, "Slowly finding my feet."

Bishop Honeywell raised an eyebrow and glanced across at Martin Fry who was putting the old man's suitcase in the boot of the car.

"And the Fry's?" he asked, "Are they looking after you?"

Archie affirmed that they were, "An absolute Godsend Your Grace, if you'll excuse the pun."

Arriving at the vicarage fifteen minutes later, Reverend Matthews led the way through the hall and into the sitting room, where he settled the Bishop into a comfortable chair.

"I'll just ask Mrs. Fry to…" he began, before realising that the housekeeper was already entering the room carrying a tray laden with coffee and biscuits.

"Milky coffee with two sugars," she smiled, setting her load down on the coffee table.

"Elizabeth!" Bishop Honeywell cried, rising from his seat and taking the woman's hands in his own, "You're looking wonderful my dear, so lovely to see you again."

Archie stood to one side looking confused. Mrs. Fry hadn't mentioned the Bishop, apart from when she'd told Archie that he covered her salary of course, and he had no idea that the two were so well acquainted.

"It seems you're familiar with each other," the vicar ventured, trying to hide his surprise, "I had no idea."

"We're old, old friends," Bishop Honeywell grinned, "And I'm looking forward to catching up properly."

"So am I," Elizabeth reciprocated, "But first get settled in and I'll make a start on lunch."

"Salmon and cucumber sandwiches?" the old man inquired, already knowing the answer.

"Of course," laughed Mrs. Fry, heading for the door, "On fresh white crusty bread."

Archie stood watching the pair smiling and laughing like a couple of children, he was certainly puzzled by the exchange but also thankful that the Bishop's familiarity with Mrs. Fry would perhaps make this visit a much more bearable one.

"So, Archibald," Bishop Honeywell said softly, as he eased himself back down into the chair, "Tell me all about your new congregation. Any problems you need my help with?"

Archie put both hands in his lap and tried not to fidget, 'I don't think so. There were a few issues in the community when I first arrived, but I think the parishioners are getting used to me know."

"And what about their secrets?" the older man asked, "Anything you can't handle? I know all about the book my son, that's why I'm here."

Archie sighed and looked up at the old man's kind eyes, "It's been a bit of a challenge," he said.

As they took a stroll around the church in the warm sun that afternoon, Reverend Matthews glowed with pride as Bishop Honeywell complimented him on a well-kept and organised establishment. In turn, Archie told him about the various issues that he'd come across, not naming anyone in particular but outlining the drinking of Marjorie Evans, the madness of Rachel Graham, Ted Bennett's scheming, the Brownlow's moonshine racket and finally the sad plight of Florence Wheeler.

"These parishioners are your test of faith Archibald," the Bishop commented when he'd heard the various stories, "God needs to know that you can help these people, and in turn they will help you."

"Me?!" Archie cried, astounded at the comment, "I don't need help Your Grace."

"We all need the support of our fellow man," Bishop Honeywell lectured, "I know what you have been through in your life, remember? I know that you need a loving community around you."

Reverend Matthews stood perplexed for a few minutes, realising that there must be a dossier on him that his seniors had read through. He wondered how in-depth the file was.

"Really, I'm alright," he said finally, "This fresh start is just what I needed."

The Bishop stood with his arms folded, looking unconvinced, "We'll see, my boy, we'll see."

As they rounded the corner of the churchyard on their path back towards the vicarage for tea, a loud rumbling suddenly started. It was followed by the groundsman coming towards them pushing a lawnmower. Archie waved at him to halt the contraption and the noise abruptly stopped.

"Good afternoon Bill," he greeted the man courteously, "I didn't realise you were working today."

"Yes, Reverend," the man replied meekly, "Sorry if I disturbed the two of you."

Bishop Honeywell stepped forward and began to inspect the mower, "Well this has certainly been in the wars," he said, tapping at the rusty handle, "What do you say we get you a new one, Mister......?"

"Wheatley," the man finished, "Bill Wheatley. That would be grand, thank you!"

Archie looked at the old man, wondering if it was his own purse strings that would need to be tightened in order to pay for the new machine, but before he could clarify the expense,

Bishop Honeywell was already heading back to the warmth of the vicarage and the steaming pot of tea that he knew would be there.

Crunching across the gravel in their leather boots, the two men walked side by side in silence. Bishop Honeywell was thinking about dinner whilst Archie was just grateful that his senior hadn't asked any questions about Mr. Wheatley. Bill, in the meantime, was oblivious to the vicar's concern, having no more cares in the world than to mow the grass in the churchyard and trim back the hedges at the vicarage.

Now Bill Wheatley was a pleasant enough fellow, who worked in whatever capacity around the church and its ground as was needed. He was chief bell-ringer, gardener, odd-job man, grave-digger and pall bearer. Never a word of complaint was uttered from his lips and, as long as his wages were paid on time, the vicar didn't hear a peep out of Bill from one week to the next. Archie hadn't noticed anything odd about Mr. Wheatley and thanked his lucky stars that he might be the one parishioner without secrets. The only slightly eccentric trait that had been noted, however, was Bill's insistence on staying in the bell tower during church service. He never, ever came out. Reverend Matthews had no idea why Bill Wheatley found it necessary to keep an eye on things in the belfry while the rest of the congregation prayed, sang and listened, but there was little that could be done to entice the man out. Archie had occasionally wondered if Bill was having a secret picnic up there on his own, or perhaps partaking of a tobacco habit but upon inspection afterwards, nothing had been out of the ordinary and not a crumb or a whiff of smoke had given a clue to the man's time up there alone.

"Does the gardener work every day?" the Bishop suddenly inquired, "I mean, does he have a day off?"

"He takes two days a week," Reverend Matthews confirmed, "Depending on what we have on."

"Ah, I see," came the slow response, "Keep an eye on him, there's a good chap."

"Why is there something I should know?" Archie queried, wondering what the old man was talking about.

"Just a gut instinct, that's all," Bishop Honeywell confided, and with that he opened the vicarage door.

Archie quickened his pace slightly to catch the door as it swung back on its hinges, "Do you think there's something odd about Bill Wheatley?"

"Well, I dare say it will come to light eventually," the minister sighed, "Can't quite put my finger on it Archibald, but there's definitely more to the man than meets the eye."

Archie immediately thought about Reverend Wilton-Hayes' black book lying on his desk.

With supper over and a couple of glasses of whisky dispensed, the Bishop hauled himself upstairs to the guest room which had been allocated to him. It was a comfortable suite, furnished in pale blue tones, and was situated at the opposite end of the upper level corridor to Archie's own room. He liked the idea of the elderly gent being over the other side of the house at night, as it would prevent him from hearing Archie call out in his sleep, which the vicar knew he inevitably would.

With Bishop Honeywell tucked up for the night, Archie turned the T.V. channel to an episode of 'Steptoe and Son,' a sitcom which he knew would help to clear his mind and relax him before he turned in for the night. Hector lay sprawled across the vicar's lap and eyed him sleepily as Archie carefully reached forward to press the television control buttons.

"It's alright," he soothed, "You can go back to sleep you lazy boy."

Hector yawned and closed his eyes, loud purring sounds vibrating from his throat. Ten minutes later his human companion was snoozing too, while the actors in the comedy carried on their antics oblivious to the vicarage and its sleeping audience.

Bang, bang, bang!

Reverend Matthews woke with a start, he'd been in a deep sleep and the noise, whatever it was, had almost made him jump out of skin. Dawn was just breaking through the flimsy green curtains and he rose to pull them back, wanting to see what the commotion was outside.

Nothing. A few birds sat contently on the garden wall and a light shone from a neighbouring barn where the farmer was bringing his herd in for milking, but there was not a single explanation for the noise. Archie rubbed at the pain in his lower back, sleeping on the sofa had worsened his already delicate spine and now a hot bath was in order. The rooms upstairs were silent as his elderly guest slept on, so tip-toeing slowly to his bathroom, Archie disrobed and waited for the steamy water to fill up. As he waited, the vicar's thoughts began to wander. The noises around the vicarage were becoming increasing louder every few days, and so far he had been unable to find a cause. Sometimes it was like gunshots, and for that he could simply put it down to poachers shooting in the fields. But on occasion he'd heard voices close by, like people rushing in blind panic. He really didn't want to entertain the idea that his new home might be haunted but Archie couldn't completely rule it out either. And today, the banging, that had been the strangest of all, closer still and like the sound of wood upon the skin of a drum.

After a leisurely breakfast of scrambled eggs on toast, courtesy of Mrs. Fry, Archie led Bishop Honeywell into his study, where he felt they could discuss parish matters in complete privacy. Assuming his role of authority, the Bishop made his way around to the far side of the desk and drew up the chair, leaving Archie to sit on a stool, feeling like a naughty schoolboy instead of the middle-aged clergy that he was. Bishop Honeywell clasped his hands together and looked down at the item on his left.

"Ah, 'The Congregation,'" he chortled, running his forefinger along the spine of the black book, "Reverend Wilton-Hayes was true to his word then."

Archie cleared his throat and attempted to show some respect to his predecessor, "It's been useful on occasion," he admitted, "Although I don't need to refer to it very often. In some cases I think the late Reverend might have exaggerated slightly."

Bishop Honeywell pondered the statement, sitting back in his seat and pulling his forefingers up to meet each other, so they resembled the steeple of a church.

"Here's the church, and there's the steeple, look inside for all the people," he muttered, acting out the popular rhyme with his fingers, wiggling them gently, "All except Bill Wheatley."

"There's nothing in the book about him," Archie interjected, "Well, nothing out of the ordinary. Bill does any jobs that need doing in and around the church, has lived on his own since his divorce in the sixties, helps out at the community centre and, of course, rings the bells as and when needed."

The Bishop frowned, waiting for more, but there wasn't anything else that the vicar could add.

"No illicit affairs or money troubles?" he asked at last.

Archie shook his head, "No. By all accounts Bill Wheatley is as clean as a whistle."

Bishop Honeywell shrugged, "Perhaps we should stop being so pessimistic about the parishioners my boy. Maybe there are one or two…"

"With all due respect…." Reverend Matthews jumped in, ready to defend the townsfolk.

But it seemed that the old man was teasing him, and laughed loudly, his flabby cheeks jiggling.

Archie couldn't help but warm to his senior, it seemed that even higher members of the church were blessed with a sense of humour too. And then he chuckled, for the first time in a long, long while.

A few days passed but the Bishop showed no signs of leaving. It wasn't that Archie was tired of the old gentleman but they seemed to have exhausted the usual parochial topics, puzzled over the parishioners and generally put the world to rights, so now he was more than ready to have his personal space back. Archie wasn't very good at dropping hints, he was much more likely to upset the Bishop by being too direct and so the week plodded along with the vicar getting frustrated and his Grace getting his feet well and truly under the proverbial table.

There was another thing that bothered Reverend Matthews too. There had been quite a few occasions over the past couple of days where he'd walked into a room where Mrs. Fry and the Bishop were chatting, only for them to immediately stop and look at him very oddly. He didn't think that his housekeeper was the kind of woman to gossip, but Archie could think of no other reason for their sly conversations, apart from himself. He wasn't bothered, but he was certainly niggled. Later that day, which happened to be Thursday, the Bishop took Archie to one side.

"Now Archibald," he said softly, resting one hand on the vicar's arm, "You will tell me if I've outstayed my welcome won't you?"

Archie flushed, "You're welcome to stay as long you as you like your Grace, but I wouldn't want you to neglect your other responsibilities on my account."

Bishop Honeywell rubbed his chin and sighed, "Ah yes, you're right, I have a good deal of other business to attend to, not least Reverend Boyle up in Maltby, now there's a parish with problems."

Archie coughed gently, "How about we get Martin to drive you to the station tomorrow morning if he's free? Most of the trains go through Maltby and they leave every hour."

"You're right my son," the Bishop conceded, "The sooner I attend to matters up there, the sooner I can get back to the comfort of my own home."

"Indeed Your Grace," Archie told him, trying to quell his excitement at the thought of his house guest leaving, "I'll check with Martin later."

"I say," the Bishop called as his younger clergy turned to put the kettle on, "Why don't we go down to the local for a couple of farewell pints tonight? It may be a while until my next visit."

Archie gritted his teeth and looked out through the kitchen window, "Yes," he replied without turning around, "That sounds like a smashing idea."

Reverend Matthews was totally unaware of how much alcohol the Bishop could withstand before it affected his ability to function normally. That evening he was about to find out.

It was a warm night with a slight breeze and the sky was still blue when they set off down the hill, two experienced clergy walking side by side, one middle-aged and one a couple of decades older. They chatted amiably about the weather, Harold Wilson the country's upright and stoic Prime Minister and trivial matters relating to the church. All in all, their arrival at 'The Swan' was uneventful.

"Evening gentlemen," Mike greeted them as he jumped off his stool, "What'll it be?"

"Pint of best bitter for me," he said pointing at the real ales, "Your Grace?"

Bishop Honeywell stood licking his lips as he perused the assortment of Scotch on the publican's top shelf. By the time Archie had his pint in front of him, the old man had decided.

"I'll sample the one at the end first," he declared, "It looks like a nice, earthy malt."

Archie was a whisky drinker but tended to stick to the same brand and couldn't comment, so instead he took a note from his pocket and laid it on the bar. It was to be the first of many rounds that he'd pay for that night.

By eleven o'clock, the time when the landlord was ready to close his doors, Archie was fairly tipsy but still able to walk in a straight line, but unfortunately Bishop Honeywell was so drunk that he was unable to focus properly, let alone hold a conversation. Archie glanced over at the malt whisky bottle which had taken the Bishop's fancy, it was almost empty, and he knew it had been full on their arrival.

"Are you able to walk Your Grace?" he asked, peering into the old clergyman's face.

"What? Waaallkk?" the Bishop slurred, patting Archie's cheek, "Of corsh I can, ha, ha."

Michael Vickers helped Reverend Matthews to put the Bishop's coat on him and the trio stumbled to the door. The publican was beaming and shaking his head.

"I know," Archie muttered, "And I've still got to get him up that darn hill yet."

"You'll be alright," Mr. Vickers joked, "The fumes will give his lordship wings!"

By the time the two clerics had struggled up to the vicarage gates, one leaning heavily on the other for support, Bishop Honeywell had started to sober up.

"I have it!" he suddenly exclaimed, "I know how we're going to trap Bill Wheatley!"

"Shush…" Archie laughed, "Tell me in the morning, we both need a good night's sleep."

Despite the intoxication and only a few hours of sleep, Archie was up bright and early the next morning. So too was Bishop Honeywell and, as Archie entered the kitchen, the unmistakable smell of bacon permeated the air. The old man was still in his dressing-gown and slippers but he appeared to be cooking breakfast for the two of them.

"Ah, there you are," the Bishop exclaimed, "Just in time my boy, take seat there's a good chap."

Archie sat at the table, where a pot of tea, toast and jams were already laid out.

"You look very chirpy Your Grace," the vicar commented, as he helped himself to milk.

"Well that's because you and I are going to solve a mystery this weekend," his companion replied excitedly, "We're going to uncover Mr. Wheatley's secret."

"We are?" Archie replied in shock, "I thought you were joking last night."

"Not at all my boy," the Bishop cackled, waving a spatula wildly, "I have an excellent plan."

As it turned out, the Bishop's plan involved him staying until the following Monday, but Archie resigned himself to a few more days of tolerable hosting for the sake of putting the old man's plan into action. They found it necessary to involve Martin Fry who, upon consultation, was more than willing to go along with the conspiracy and he in turn told Elizabeth who agreed to keep things under wraps.

To execute their actions, Bishop Honeywell insisted upon taking the Sunday Service that weekend, leaving Reverend Matthews free to investigate the strange goings-on in the bell tower, where he suspected Bill Wheatley was involved in some tryst. Martin Fry was to stay outside in the graveyard and keep a watchful eye on any sudden attempts to escape. Elizabeth thought it a plan full of holes, but none of the men took a blind bit of notice and insisted upon executing their deed at once.

As the congregation filed into the church, excited at the prospect of receiving a sermon from the Bishop himself, Bill Wheatley was in the belfry, ringing the bells to welcome the flock. He was assisted by several other members of the community but, as Archie noted from his position near the font, when the chiming stopped, the other campanologists took their seats to join the service. Mr. Wheatley did not.

Waiting until the first hymn began, so that the other parishioners were preoccupied with displaying their vocal skills to the Bishop, Archie carefully turned the handle on the door to the bell tower and slipped inside. As he did so, there was a gentle click on the opposite side exit and a certain gentleman hurried out. Archie followed, stepping carefully to avoid his shoes clicking on the flagstones, and just caught sight of Bill Wheatley's jacket disappearing from view.

The vicar looked around. Martin Fry was near the low stone wall signaling for him to go that way, so Archie hitched up his cassock like a billowing dress, and ran across the graveyard at full pelt.

"Come on," Martin puffed, "He's on his bike, heading towards town. Get in the car."

Archie followed Mr. Fry's willowy figure to the Ford Cortina and jumped in the passenger's side.

"Cor blimey," Martin wheezed, "I haven't run like that since senior school sports day."

"Well, perhaps now you'll think about giving up those ghastly cigarettes," Archie lectured, pulling at his seatbelt.

The driver shot him a dirty look and started the engine, "Do you want me to follow him or not?"

"Yes, yes," the vicar huffed, flapping his hands, "Hurry up or we'll lose him."

Downhill they drove, keeping a safe enough distance for the unsuspecting Mr. Wheatley not to notice, but close enough to see where he went. It wasn't long until the middle-aged man on the bicycle stopped and dismounted, leaving his stead propped up against a nearby wall. Martin pulled up behind a parked car and the two men watched as Bill adjusted his tie and combed the few stands of greying hair up and over his head, smoothing them into place with a dab of spit on his hand.

"He's got a woman," Mr. Fry murmured excitedly, "Look he's going up the garden path."

"Ooh, so he is," Archie answered in a low voice, "We'd better wait here. And why are we whispering?"

Just a few minutes later, Bill Wheatley reappeared, looking a little flushed and pushing something deep into his jacket pocket.

Archie and Martin looked at one another, puzzled.

"Well he hasn't had long enough to…erm, you know," the driver began.

"How long does it take?" Archie asked, not realising the implications of his question.

Martin nudged him in the ribs, looking like he was about to make a joke and then he changed his mind.

"Oh bugger," he said, looking slightly embarrassed, "I forgot you were a vicar for a minute!"

"Yes, well, never mind," Archie flapped, "He's off again, come on."

A few streets later Bill stopped again, carefully getting off his bike, smoothing down his hair and going up the entrance of a semi-detached house. It was hard to see what he was doing but the vicar was sure that the strange man was heading for the back of the house. He emerged once again, after just a few minutes and stood on the street fussing with the contents of his pockets once again.

"Right, next house, you need to get out and follow him," Martin Fry declared, stabbing Archie with his finger, "Otherwise we'll be here all day and none the wiser."

"Me?" Archie exclaimed, his voice rising, "Why me? Besides, I'm wearing my gown and I can hardly run around in it. You'll have to go."

"Oh no I won't," his friend argued, "I need to be ready in case we have to make a quick getaway."

"Very well," Archie huffed, trying to pull the cassock up over his head, "Just don't lose him."

As the Cortina crawled along the streets, following their un-suspecting prey to a myriad of garden gates, several teenagers stopped to stare. It must have been quite a sight too, with Martin Fry hunched over the wheel, a cigarette hanging from the cor-ner of his mouth, whilst the cloth-covered passenger struggled to get undressed. As for Bill Wheatley, he continued to jump off his bicycle at regular intervals, comb his wild hair and re-mained obsessed with the contents of his pockets, oblivious to his followers.

"Quick, quick," Mr. Fry shouted, pulling the car to a halt, "Get out, he's gone up there."

Archie shoved the black tunic into the back of the car and scrambled out. He could see Bill sauntering up another garden path and stealthily crept along the hedgerow on the other side. As he neared the end, where the bushes reached a fence, the vicar poked his head up over the brambles.

It was then that he witnessed Bill Wheatley's secret.

The strange man was standing in the garden of the house, staring at the washing-line. He was transfixed, with a wide grin on his face. Suddenly he dashed forward and grabbed a pair of silky knickers off the line, stuffing them deep into his jacket lin-ing as he ran back towards his bike.

Archie stooped down and tried to scramble quickly back to the car but his back started to ache under all the activity and the best he could do was a slow crawl.

By the time they arrived back at the church, both the vicar and the housekeeper's husband were looking a little worse for wear. Archie had patches of mud on his dark trousers and the cassock was creased up like an old tissue. Martin looked alright on first glance, but there was shock in his eyes at the latest revelation. Service was coming to an end, and Bishop Honeywell read the final prayer, with just enough time for Bill Wheatley to slip back inside the belfry and take his place underneath the bells.

Bishop Honeywell stood in the fresh air watching the congregation leave, his brow was furrowed.

"A panty pincher eh?" he grumbled, "It has to stop you know."

Archie agreed, feeling a little shudder go down his spine as he thought about Bill Wheatley's collection of freshly laundered underwear.

"So, what do I do?" he asked, gently brushing at the mud on his sleeves.

"Do, my boy?" the Bishop laughed, "Why you preach to the women next Sunday Archibald, about the sins of doing their washing on the Lord's day of rest."

Archie winked, "I think I can manage that," he said.

Chapter Eight

The Trubshaw Family

It was the third Sunday in June and Reverend Matthews was preparing for a Christening that would take place within the usual Sunday Service. It was the first one he'd had to conduct since moving to the town and he felt very agitated. You see, the vicar wasn't particularly tolerant of children, he hadn't really had much contact with them within his own family and the youngsters who attended church annoyed him with their constant fidgeting and complaining. Christenings were the bane of his life, he just knew that the baby being blessed would cry the minute he splashed water over its head. On more than one occasion in his previous parish the little tykes had wet themselves as the first icy trickle made contact and he had found himself in a most disagreeable predicament. Archie hoped that today would not be one of those days.

The service progressed at its usual pace and the congregation sang with gusto. Reverend Matthews had chosen 'Onward Christian Soldiers' and 'The Old Rugged Cross' for the first two hymns and, being the most popular songs, everyone sang their hearts out. As the parishioners stood, open-mouthed, holding their hymn books, the vicar looked around. He felt immense pride that week after week the turnout at church was growing and more and more people were becoming involved in the parish activities. Doctor Evans, for example, had volunteered to join the choir and his deep baritone voice was absolutely pitch perfect. There was still no sign of Marjorie Evans attending regular church services, however, but she did make the occasional appearance at a wedding, christening or funeral, where she knew that the alcohol would be free-flowing afterwards.

Rachel Graham seemed to be coping well and would regularly be seen helping her imaginary friends into a pew and passing them a service sheet. Ted Bennett never missed a Sunday nowadays, and he was always first to reach deep into his pockets to make a donation to the collection plate.

After the termination of their moonshine racket, the Brownlow family had made an extra effort to join the flock, their teenage children tagging along reluctantly but always smartly dressed and respectable. Of course Florence Wheeler was a key member of the congregation now, sitting perched on the front row with her handbag clutched tightly on her knees and her husband snuggled in affectionately beside her. They still brought flowers for the children's graves half an hour before service began, saying silent prayers for their loss and tidying up any weeds or overgrown grass as they did so.

Bill Wheatley had taken the hint about washing-lines after a couple of weeks, and now watched proceedings from the back of the church. Seemingly no more underwear had disappeared.

And so today, with the congregation looking on, their faces smiling and cooing over little baby Trubshaw, the babe in arms waiting to be Christened, Reverend Matthews requested the family to gather around the font. Mrs. Fry was on hand to help and dutifully gave out candles to the chosen godparents, who stood resplendent in their best suits and flouncy dresses, eyes all transfixed on the infant.

Mr. and Mrs. Trubshaw were looking particularly well turned out and Archie expected that there would be a fancy party to celebrate their child's christening afterwards. He knew that heavily set Barry Trubshaw was a long-distance lorry driver and spent days at a time away from home, while Stephanie, his wife, had worked a few odd shifts at 'The Swan' until she'd fallen pregnant the previous summer. They were a young couple, in their mid-twenties, and little Isobel was their first-born. A blonde, delicate baby, with dark hazel eyes, Archie couldn't help but think the child's colouring a very unusual combination as both parents had mousy brown hair and blue eyes. Still, he had no prior knowledge of the couple as they'd moved to the town quite recently, therefore evading Reverend Wilton-Hayes' scrutiny in that thick black chronicle.

Lifting Isobel Trubshaw carefully into his arms, and mentally cursing the copious layers of lace on the baby's gown, Reverend Matthews scooped a cupful of water from the font with his free hand and blessed the child in a strong, clear voice. There was no screaming, just a gentle smile as the little girl gazed up into the vicar's eyes. Archie couldn't help but smile back, his defensive wall crumbling slightly, and the baby giggled joyously.

After the service, Barry Trubshaw approached the vicar to thank him.

"You've got a real knack with babies," he smiled, shaking Archie's hand enthusiastically.

"I'm out of practice I'm afraid," Reverend Matthews blushed, "But she's a very good girl."

Mr. Trubshaw pointed over at his wife, "Takes after her mother, she's a diamond." He paused for a moment, to watch Stephanie rock their child to sleep in her pram, and then turned back to Archie.

"You will come to 'The Swan' for a drink and the buffet won't you vicar?"

Reverend Matthews glanced at his watch. If he stopped for a couple of hours, he'd still be back at the vicarage in time for University Challenge on television. Archie's favourite part of the week was pitting his knowledge against those super-intelligent boffins.

"Absolutely," he replied, "But just for a while, I have lots of things to attend to Mr. Trubshaw."

The chubby man nodded and crunched over the gravel to his circle of friends and family. Archie watched him walk away and couldn't help but think there was something rather unusual about Barry Trubshaw but before any ideas could get deeply implanted in his head, the vicar cursed his suspicious mind and told himself to stop over-thinking things. The Trubshaws were decent, happy and normal.

Down at 'The Swan', Michael Vickers and his staff were busy pulling pints and setting out paper plates with folded napkins between each one. Archie had often wondered why people did that. It annoyed him terribly, because he was the type of slightly messy eater who might require more than one napkin and he'd always wondered about the etiquette of going back for a second one, should one take the second plate as well or leave it 'napkinless' for another diner? As he pondered this question now, as he had done on many an occasion before, Barry Trubshaw appeared at Archie's side with two pints of beer.

"Mr. Vickers said you drink best bitter," the young man beamed, handing the vicar a foaming glass, "Get that down you Reverend."

"Oh, really," Archie flushed, taking the beer, "There was no need. And thank you again for inviting me."

Barry Trubshaw looked down at his shiny black shoes, trying to think of something to say. He wasn't used to talking to religious men and felt a bit embarrassed that he didn't know the parish vicar better.

Archie stood looking at the man's rosy cheeks and smooth complexion, subconsciously running a hand over his own two day growth of stubble. He'd forgotten to shave that morning.

"Well, I'd better go and say hello to your wife," the vicar said eventually, breaking the silence, "And I see little Isobel's still sound asleep."

Barry breathed out slowly, glad of the reprieve, "Yes, I'll take her out for some fresh air."

The two men walked over to Stephanie Trubshaw, Archie starting a conversation about how well-behaved the baby had been during her dunking in the font and Barry wheeling his baby's pram out through the back door, away from the smoke and loud chatter.

As he had already promised himself, Archie set off back home after an hour and a half, thinking of nothing but putting his feet up on the sofa with Hector, while testing his wits against the brains on T.V.

Hector was already waiting, with three mice, all dead, lying on the bristly mat by the door.

The following day Reverend Matthews was in a very sombre mood. It was the anniversary of his beloved grandmother's death, many years ago now but still raw and painful, so he decided to take an hour to himself, praying and thinking. As usual on a Monday morning the church was quiet and empty, the flowers from yesterday's service were in full bloom and the delightful aroma of lilies filled the air. Archie eased himself down onto the front row pew and propped his precious childhood photograph up on the wooden ledge in front of him. He ran a solitary finger across the smiling face of his sibling, the happy go lucky look of a child without a care in the world, and then bowed his head to pray for his grandma and brother.

Some time later, feeling slightly better, the vicar rose and tucked the precious photograph into his jacket pocket and headed towards the belfry, wanting to check that everything was in order after the previous day's service. He still felt wary of Bill Wheatley's shenanigans. However, before he could get to the door of the bell tower, Archie noticed a small circular object lying by the font. Stooping down for closer inspection he discovered that it was a tiny mitten, more than likely belonging to the babe in arms whom he had christened the day before. He picked it up and walked outside.

The morning was warm with just a few greying clouds rolling towards the hills in the distance, nothing to be concerned about. The vicar looked down at the tiny mitten, soft to the touch and threaded with pink ribbon, it felt softer than a cotton ball. Glancing back up at the sky, he resolved to deliver the item to its owner, besides a good stroll into town might lift his spirits somewhat. Therefore, sliding the mitten into the opposite pocket to the one which held the photograph, he slipped through the church gates and set off towards town. No doubt Mrs. Fry would be wondering where he was, fretting over some meal she had ready for his lunch, but Archie had no appetite that day, worrying instead about his brother's unkempt grave all those miles away.

After calling round to the back door of 'The Swan' to get directions to the Trubshaw residence from Mike Vickers, Reverend Matthews plodded along until he came to a couple of farm cottages on the road to the mine. Both looked well cared for and the gardens were just coming into bloom. The one rented by Barry Trubshaw and his family was on the left as he looked at them and brilliant white net curtains hung from each window, gleaming like angel's wings. The vicar ran a hand through his soft silvery hair and bent down to undo the latch on the little metal gate. He then stopped to listen, making sure that no roaming dog was about to come and bite his ankles. Certain that he had nothing to fear, Archie knocked on the door.

"Reverend, good morning," Stephanie Trubshaw said enthusiastically as she opened the door, bouncing baby Isobel up and down on her hip as she did so, "What a nice surprise."

Archie reached into his pocket and pulled out the folded cloth, "Hello Mrs. Trubshaw, I found this."

Stephanie let out a girly giggle and reached out to take her daughter's tiny mitten, "Ha, I was wondering where that went to, pretty much turned the house upside down looking for it."

"Oh well, sorry about that," the vicar sighed, "It was in the church, next to the font."

"Time for a cup of tea?" the woman offered, opening the door wider, "Kettle's already on."

Archie hesitated for a second and then conceded, "Yes, thank you, tea would be lovely."

The cottage kitchen was warm and inviting, with a small oil-burning Rayburn permanently set on low to help dry washing and also to warm the rest of the house. A long over-head airer was positioned above the stove and the vicar could see that on this particular day it was being put to good use. Although many of the items being dried looked like large women's girdles.

Stephanie passed her baby to Archie while she prepared their drinks and he held the little girl gently but awkwardly. Isobel seemed quite happy to sit upon the vicar's lap and cooed up at him while exploring his buttons with her nimble fingers. Archie took in his surroundings while he waited for the tea, looking down at the baby every minute or so, just to ensure that she was content.

It appeared that Mrs. Trubshaw kept a neat enough house although, had Archie lived here, the babies milk bottles and their cleaning equipment would have been tidied away instead of cluttering up the work surfaces. He noticed sprinkles of sugar on the table too, where someone had obviously spilled it when making their drink, and the upright swing bin seemed to be rather full too. The vicar sniffed, he could smell something like dog food wafting across the room, mingled with the distinctive smell of a clean baby. He looked down at his lap, Isobel's chubby arms showed traces of baby powder and her hair was soft and fluffy, the tell-tale sign of it being freshly washed.

He jiggled the baby girl up and down on the edge of his knee a couple of times, trying to make her giggle and immediately succeeding. Archie made first contact with Isobel's eyes, dark and beady like brown marbles, and, for the second time in as many days, wondered about the child's unusual colouring.

"Here let me take Isobel," Stephanie offered, setting down two mugs of tea, "She's probably ready for her nap now anyway."

Archie dutifully passed the little girl to her mother, a smile playing on his lips as he did so.

"There we go," he sighed, "Off to beddy byes little one."

"I won't be a minute," Mrs. Trubshaw told him, "Help yourself to biscuits from the barrel."

The vicar looked at the silver and wood container on the table and noticed that the lid was only half on, he presumed that the contents might be soft or stale by now and turned his attention to the tea.

As the young woman left the room, Archie used the opportunity of being alone to take in his surroundings properly. The first thing that caught the vicar's eye was a small stack of cookery books, all borrowed from the library, showing small whited code stickers on their spines and all offering basic recipes for pastry, cakes, stews and puddings. The young housewife was obviously trying to improve her culinary skills. The vicar's stomach gave an involuntary rumble as he wondered what delights Mrs. Fry would be conjuring up for him, she really was such an excellent cook. Trying to quell his growing appetite, Archie blew gently on his hot tea and let the liquid slide down his throat. In raising the mug upwards, his eyes were once again drawn to the garments that were drying over the top of the stove. The large corsets certainly couldn't belong to Stephanie, she had far too slender a frame, perhaps she took in washing for others or had an elderly relative to care for Archie wondered.

"All tucked up and nodding off," Mrs. Trubshaw announced, coming back into the room.

"Ah, good," Reverend Matthews nodded, "You might get an hour or so to yourself now then."

The young woman smiled and pointed towards the recipe books, "I was hoping to have enough time to make something special for our tea tonight, it's mine and Barry's anniversary."

"Lovely," Archie enthused, setting down his empty mug, "How many years have you been married, if you don't mind me asking?"

Stephanie blushed, a rosy glow flooding to her cheeks as soon as the question was asked, "We've been together five years vicar."

Archie sensed a slight quaver in her voice but the woman was still smiling.

At a loose end later that afternoon, having succumbed to a plate of cheese and pickle sandwiches and a slice of his housekeeper's excellent fruit cake, Archie wandered over to the church to make a list of tasks that needed attending to. It was still fairly warm outside but the inside of the building was as cold as ice, as usual. The vicar cursed himself at not having brought a jacket, he was bound to suffer an aching spine after an hour or so in these temperatures, he told himself.

The urge to keep warm spurred Reverend Matthews into action, and within thirty minutes he'd managed to write a substantial list, enough to keep him busy for several weeks in fact. The only nook he hadn't considered was the vestry, which is where his feet now stepped towards.

It was slightly warmer, due to the compact size and velvet drapes, and housed the vicar's various ceremonial robes. This was also where he kept the most valuable religious artifacts, safely under lock and key. After all, you never knew when a member of the flock might be led into temptation. One item that wasn't locked away was the parish register, a heavy, cumbersome book in which generations of vicars had faithfully recorded the deaths, marriages and christenings of the towns-folk. Archie sat down in a ladder-back chair and pulled the chronicle towards him, automatically flicking back to five years previously. If the Trubshaws had married in this district, he told himself, the date would be in here. Instinct had convinced him that there was more to Stephanie and Barry's relationship than he realised, and curiosity was now beginning to get the better of him.

Nothing. No record of the bans being read and certainly no marriage. Still, it could only be concluded that the couple had moved here more recently than he had first assumed. Archie wondered if Mrs. Fry would be forthcoming with more details if he pressed her, however it wasn't the case.

"Mrs. Fry," Reverend Matthews began, just as the middle-aged woman was leaving for the day, "Do you know the Trubshaws? They seem like a nice young couple."

Elizabeth continued to pull on her cotton jacket without turn-ing around, "Yes, they're lovely."

"Did they move here recently?" he pressed, trying desperately to sound casual.

"Yes, only a couple of years ago, if my memory serves me cor-rectly," Elizabeth replied, now turning to lift her handbag from the back of the door, "Why?"

Archie shrugged, "Oh, no reason in particular, I just wondered where they held their wedding ceremony."

"What a strange thing to be thinking about," the housekeeper commented, "What's wrong?"

"Nothing," he lied, "It's just that it's their anniversary today."

"Oh," came the terse response, "Well, I guess that's their busi-ness isn't it?"

Archie took a step towards Mrs. Fry, intending to see if she was upset about something, as her voice certainly didn't sound friendly and the sharp look she had given him could have turned his rice pudding to ice, but a second later she was gone, slamming the door behind her.

That evening, stretched out on the sofa with Hector, the vicar took out his pocket diary with the intention of copying down his list of jobs to be done in the church. He figured that if he set his mind to tackling one large or a two small items every week, the vast area would be ship-shape in time for Christmas. Luckily the vicarage itself was under the close scrutiny of his housekeeper and therefore he needed to do very little in the way of maintenance at home. Flicking to the day's date, Archie poised his pencil and prepared to write. Bugger, he cursed, that's what was wrong!

Staring at him from the page, written in his own clear cursive hand, on that very day was Mrs. Fry's birthday. Archie moaned inwardly. Of all the people whom he could really count on, The Frys were top of the list. They'd given him every assistance in settling in, organised lifts from one place to another, brought him hot meals from their own kitchen, rallied around on Sundays but most importantly of all, Martin and Elizabeth had given him friendship.

The vicar ran upstairs immediately, hoping that perhaps something could be salvaged of the situation after all. Opening his beside cabinet, Archie knelt down and lifted something from inside. It was a beautiful pink cashmere scarf, recently purchased from one of the larger stores in town, and an item that had been intended for his mother's birthday the following week.

"I can always buy mummy another one in time to post it," he muttered, racing back downstairs to find a piece of wrapping paper, "My absentmindedness shall certainly cost me."

As it happened, delivering Elizabeth's gift to her that evening turned out to open up a can of worms that even Reverend Matthews didn't know how to keep the lid on!

"Thank you," Mrs. Fry squealed excitedly as she tore open her present on the front doorstep like a young child, "I really thought you'd forgotten, but then again you really shouldn't have...."

Archie coughed, slightly embarrassed that his gesture had caused such a reaction, "Just a token of my appreciation Mrs. Fry."

"Oh will you stop being so formal," the woman giggled, throwing her arms around the vicar's neck, "You need to start calling me Elizabeth."

"Very well, if you wish," he nodded, wondering how to detach himself politely.

"Where are my manners?! Please come in," Mrs. Fry continued, suddenly letting go of her employer, "Martin's just about to open a bottle of wine."

"That's very kind," Archie conceded, "But I was rather hoping for a hot bath and an early night."

Elizabeth stood back, looking at him in the knowing way that she always did, understanding his need for space and solitude, "Of course. Goodnight then vicar."

"Archie," he replied, letting his guard down for a split second, "I'll see you in the morning Elizabeth."

"Goodnight," she grinned, preparing to go inside, but then hesitating slightly and calling out once more, "By the way, what you asked me about earlier, the Trubshaws aren't married."

The enormity of that one sentence didn't fully impact Reverend Matthews until the next day. He'd mulled over the implications of his housekeeper's comment of course, but these were the 1970's and plenty of young people were taking the bold step of living together before exchanging vows. He wasn't adverse to the idea, despite its non-conformity to his own beliefs but bringing up a child out of wedlock was quite a different matter altogether and it bothered the vicar immensely. It was such a shame that young Isobel hadn't been born of such a union, although Archie had absolutely no doubt that the Trubshaws were completely devoted to each other. There was only one thing for it, he would have to speak to them. A friendly word and some gentle persuasion may be all that was necessary after all, and if it was a case of being short of money, he could always talk to Mike Vickers at The Swan about…it was then that the vicar stopped planning. Of course Barry and Stephanie could afford to get married, he realised, they had spent enough on little Isobel's christening. Maybe they just didn't want to. He'd soon change that!

As part of his strategy to convince Barry and Stephanie Trubshaw of the importance of wedlock, Reverend Matthews took the bull by the horns on Sunday and prepared a sermon about Adam and Eve, the way in which they were created in the eyes of the Lord and the myriad of temptations laid bare before them. With subtle prose and delicate manipulation, the vicar managed to swing the conclusion around to the sanctity of marriage and how couples should look upon their relationships as a long-term investment, ultimately sent by God to test them.

The lecture was well received by all, as it happened, including the couple for which it was intended. Now, standing in the summer sun, shaking hands with the parishioners and enjoying some warmth on his face, Archie found himself eye to eye with Barry Trubshaw.

"That was a great service vicar," complimented the younger man, "I was just saying to Linda that everything you said made sense, about the importance of relationships and the like."

This was music to the clergyman's ears and he took Barry by the elbow, leading him to one side.

"Mr. Trubshaw, I'm so glad you see the relevance of today's sermon, you see there's a delicate matter I'd like to discuss with you."

Barry listened intently as the vicar continued.

"You see, I happen to know that you and Stephanie aren't married, and I wondered if there might be some reason or complication that I could assist with, you see…"

Archie stopped. Barry Trubshaw had raised a hand to his head and was rubbing his eyes, trying desperately not to cry.

"Sorry vicar, it's time we were getting back, Isobel will need her feed shortly."

Reverend Matthews watched the other man walk away, his cheeks flushed and head bowed, and wondered if he'd really upset the applecart this time. He hadn't meant to cause upset.

Feeling a hand on his shoulder, Archie glanced to his side and found Martin Fry standing there.

"There's not much you can say to youngsters these days vicar, without them going off on one."

"I just sense there's more to it than meets the eye," Archie confessed, "They both seem so sensible."

Mr. Fry lit a cigarette and raised an eyebrow, "I'm sure you'll figure it out," he said.

For the next couple of days, Reverend Matthews pondered on his encounter and chided himself. Perhaps he'd gone about things entirely the wrong way, he mused, jumping in with both feet before trying the subtle approach. He just didn't get it, Barry Trubshaw himself had admitted that he agreed with the words spoken in church, surely that meant that he supported the idea of taking Stephanie as his wife. Still, it wasn't in the vicar's nature to tell others how to live their lives, he didn't feel he had a right to that given his own shortcomings, but he desperately hoped that his clumsy lecture hadn't caused a rift in the congregation.

Five days passed before Archie was to come into contact with the Trubshaw's again, and surprisingly it was they who appeared on the vicarage doorstep. Mrs. Fry had already left for the day, indeed perhaps the couple already knew that and had waited until the vicar was alone, therefore Archie was obliged to answer the doorbell himself, a chore that he rarely participated in when his housekeeper was there. He peered through the frosted glass in the front door and recognised the pair at once.

"Why, good afternoon," he declared, pulling the door wide open, "Please do come in."

The Trubshaws followed Reverend Matthews down the hallway to the sitting room, chattering politely about the weather and how it had taken a turn for the better.

"And Isobel? I notice she's not with you," Archie observed.

"She's with Mrs. Wheeler," Stephanie informed him, "Just for a while, so that we could speak to you."

"I see, well, do sit down. How can I help?"

Now, despite his calm demeanour, the vicar was already preparing himself to be told that the couple wanted to set a date for their wedding, and fidgeted in his chair.

"Look, the thing is Reverend," Barry Trubshaw began, "We know you mean well, what with your sermon and all those hints you've been dropping, but the thing is, we're in love but we can't get married."

Archie sat completely still, his mouth forming an 'O', before pressing on with his enquiry.

"Is there some legal reason? Are one of you married to someone else?" he asked, sincerely hoping that this was most definitely not the case.

"No, nothing like that," Stephanie interjected shyly, looking at her partner, "Neither of us are married."

The vicar smiled warmly, genuinely wanting to help, "Come then, surely we can overcome whatever it is."

The couple sat silently, blinking at each other and avoiding the clergyman's gaze. Eventually Barry took a deep breath and poured out their troubles.

"Isobel isn't mine," he confessed, reaching for Stephanie's hand, "She's my brother's child."

Archie sat in shock, taking in the enormity of the other man's words. "I see," was all he could manage.

"I'm afraid you don't," Mr. Trubshaw continued, "Stephanie and Ralph had my full consent."

Archie ran his fingers through his hair and stood up, "I don't think I should hear any more......"

'Please," Stephanie entreated him, "Please listen to what we have to tell you."

Archie sat down on the arm of his chair, ready to rise again if necessary, "Alright, go on."

"You see we desperately wanted a child of our own," Barry admitted, "But I can't have any."

"But surely there's adoption," Archie blurted, "Or fostering, even."

"It's not an option for us vicar, you see we're not a conventional kind of couple."

Archie still didn't understand what they were trying to say, "So, what kind of couple are you?"

Stephanie sighed, frustrated that it was taking so long for the Reverend to latch on, "Barry was born Brenda," she said, laying all her cards on the table at once.

The vicar reeled, he truly was astounded. But then it suddenly dawned on him, all the signs had been there. The smooth complexion, the mild mannerisms, even the large corsets hanging up to dry in their little cottage kitchen. Barry Trubshaw was still, physically, a woman.

"Of course, we'll move away if it's an issue," Stephanie offered, "We couldn't ask you to keep it a secret."

The vicar breathed through his nose, slowly and purposely, watching the faces of a couple who loved each other unreservedly despite the odds and prejudices around them.

"Your secret's safe with me," he said finally, "I'm a man of God, and I'll keep my word."

Chapter Nine

Romana and Magdalena Getzi

As the height of summer spread its warm sunny wings across the town, Reverend Matthews found himself looking upon his duties to the parishioners akin to that of a shepherd tending his flock. There would always be the black sheep amongst them, those who had difficulty in leading a pure and honest life but he had to admit, all in all, the townsfolk were generous, caring and kind, those whose acquaintance he had met, at least. Now upon the subject of people whom the vicar had not yet met, there were only a few. Some lesser known citizens had still raised their hand in seeing the clergyman pass or slid into the back pew at church quite late and left as soon as service was over, but there were few whose lives still remained a mystery to him. However, amongst those who never ever came to church were the Getzi sisters.

Archie had first heard about them at the beginning of August, almost eight months into his tenancy at the vicarage and at a time when he and Mrs. Fry had become much more comfortable in one another's company, the latter now sharing a joke or snippet of gossip with her employer at regular intervals. As it happened, on this particular morning as Elizabeth recounted one of the congregation's antics, the doorbell rang. As the housekeeper was up to her elbows in soapy water at the sink, the vicar raised his hand and headed down the hallway to answer it, still chuckling to himself as he went.

"Morning old chap," smiled Doctor Evans, stepping over the threshold without waiting to be invited, "I wondered if there might be a cup of coffee on offer, cheeky of me I know but I was passing and…"

"Of course," Archie shrugged, leading the way to the kitchen, "Follow me."

"Actually, could we drink it in the study?" the medical man whispered, "I've got a rather delicate matter I'd like to discuss with you."

"Absolutely," the vicar replied, "Sit yourself down and I'll ask Elizabeth to prepare a tray."

"Elizabeth, eh?" the doctor snorted, patting Archie on the back.

"We have a purely platonic relationship," Archie shot back indignantly, "Nothing wrong with being on first name terms, we do have to work closely together almost every day of the week."

"Of course you do," Dr. Evans chortled, "And some evenings too I'll bet."

Archie ignored the last comment and hurried off down the corridor wishing now that he'd pretended not to hear the bell.

"So, what was so important to cause you to call in?" Reverend Matthews asked, coming straight to the point as he closed the study door behind him.

"Well, as I said, it's a very delicate matter," the doctor began, folding his hands across one knee, "I'm in quite a quandary about one of my patients."

"Oh? Do go on," Archie responded, taking the opposite armchair, "Anyone I know?"

"Well, I'm not sure," Doctor Evans said slowly, scratching his head, "It's Romana Getzi."

Archie shook his head, not recognising the name.

"She lives with her sister Magdalena. They rent a little cottage up on Dashbury Moor, about three miles past Brushfield Farm."

"Sorry," Archie admitted, "Never heard of them."

The medic leaned forward and exhaled before continuing, "They're Hungarian I think, both well into their seventies and pretty much self-sufficient, growing most of their own produce. Nobody knows how long they've been living up there, or where they came from exactly, but it must be twenty years or more."

"And this one sister, Romana, she's unwell you say?" the vicar clarified.

"Yes, just a case of gastroenteritis," the doctor told him, "I've given her some medication. However, there's something very mysterious going on in that cottage, and I can't fathom what it is."

Just then there was a knock on the door and Mrs. Fry entered with coffee and biscuits.

"I'll leave you to help yourselves," she said politely, backing out into the hall, "I'll be upstairs hoovering if you need me vicar."

Archie smiled and turned his attention back to the matter at hand, "What kind of mysterious thing are you talking about? You know I'll help if I can."

For the next half an hour he listened intently as Doctor Evans explained the dilemma.

That afternoon, Archie paced the church aisle, thinking about the information that Dr. Evans had given him about the Getzi sisters. Personally, he couldn't see why his friend was so worked up, although some details were a little odd and hard to explain away lightly. The matter would have to be handled tactfully and subtly he decided, and a vicar was quite possibly the best person to undertake such a task. As he strode up and down, watching the sun flicker against the stained-glass windows, Archie struck upon a plan of action that involved the assistance of Mrs. Fry.

"Elizabeth," he said, rinsing his hands under the tap as the housekeeper rolled pastry at the worktop, "Do you have enough apples to make an extra pie by any chance?"

Mrs. Fry peered into the wicker basket on the floor and nodded, "I should think so, who's it for?"

"The two old women up on Dashbury Moor," he confessed, wondering if she might change her mind.

"Oh. Okay," she replied, sprinkling flour onto the rolling pin, "Are you taking it up there yourself?"

"Yes, I was planning to."

"I'll bring Martin's pushbike over for you," Elizabeth offered, still not turning around, "But be careful to come back before dusk, it can get very foggy up on those moors."

"What, in summer?" Archie laughed.

"Yes, even in summer," she warned, "And don't forget to wear your cross."

The vicar scowled, wondering why on earth Mrs. Fry was being so dramatic, but he was unable to see her biting her lip as she worked at the pastry, desperately holding back a fit of uncontrollable laughter.

At quarter past four, fifteen minutes after finishing work for the day, Elizabeth Fry returned to the vicarage pushing her husband's bicycle. It looked fairly new and modern, with a rectangular rack over the back wheel designed for carrying small parcels and a cross-bar running from the seat to the handlebars, making it what Archie would describe 'a racing bike'. At first he struggled to get the hang of riding with his back arched over, not a position that he found either comfortable nor practical, but after a few hundred yards down the lane he began to feel more relaxed and enjoyed the countryside around him.

As he neared the cottage, the first thing that became apparent to the vicar was that the Getzi sisters cottage was built in the style of a crofter's cottage, such as found gracing the hills in the Scottish Highlands. The natural stone had been whitewashed but the original wooden door had a dull and rough appearance, as though it had weathered many storms. There was a slow trickle of grey curling smoke wafting up from the central chimney, causing Reverend Matthews to stop and stare. Sweat had gathered under his armpits, which was more to do with the warm afternoon than the exertion of cycling, causing Archie to wonder just how cold it was inside the stone cottage that its occupants needed to light a fire. He carefully dismounted, wheeling the bicycle up to the wall surrounding the cottage garden and began to untie the apple pie from its location on the parcel rack.

"Who is coming?" came a sharp voice from the doorway.

The vicar jumped slightly, he hadn't even heard the door open.

"Ah Ms. Gertz?" he asked, coming face to face with a very short wizened old woman wearing a white apron over her dark clothing, "I'm Reverend Matthews. Just stopped by to see how you are."

"Get, zee, Getzi," the pensioner corrected, "Why you come here?"

Archie strained to make out the strong foreign accent and realised that there might well be a communication breakdown shortly, "To see you. I'm the vicar."

"Humph," the woman snorted, "Vee, car, we no need."

"I'm a friend of Doctor Evans," he said quickly as Ms. Getzi started to close the door, "I've brought you a fresh apple pie."

The Hungarian stopped, hovering on the step and sniffing the air like a wolf, "Is good?" she asked.

"Oh yes, very good indeed," Archie promised.

The woman turned to go back inside but beckoned with her free hand, "Come, I make tea."

Archie stepped into a large kitchen, where the heat from the fire was stiflingly warm, but made even more intense by the low ceiling and heavy drapes. Ms. Getzi didn't speak, but occupied herself with filling a large black kettle. She then carefully lifted a huge bubbling pot from the hearth and replaced it with the kettle.

"Is that your supper?" Reverend Matthews asked cheerfully, trying to lighten the mood, "Smells lovely."

The old lady blinked and looked at the pot. She then let out a cackling laugh, the likes of which Archie had never heard before, showing her toothless gums and bright red tongue.

"Is stocking," she finally managed, catching her breath.

"Sorry?" Archie said, looking confused.

"In pot, is stocking," Ms. Getzi repeated, but then realising that the vicar didn't understand, she took a pair of long wooden laundry tongs and lifted a thick woollen stocking out of the pot, "I do wash."

Archie nodded, feeling quite foolish, and then remembered the pie that he was still holding.

"There we are," he said slowly, trying to make it easier for the old lady to comprehend, "Apple pie."

"I not deaf," she snapped, inspecting the pastry, "I Magda."

For the next ten minutes, conversation was very stilted. Archie went through all the usual niceties, talking about the weather, the church and general news, all the time trying to swallow the terrible tasting dishwater that Magda Getzi had insisted was tea. He vaguely suspected that she had given him some weird out-of-date Eastern European concoction instead of proper English tea, but he did his best to drink it with a strained amount of pleasantry.

"Who is coming?" another voice interrupted, "I no see car."

The vicar swivelled around on his stool to see who was speaking and immediately saw an identical Getzi twin walking into the room. She was just as short, with the same sparkly eyes and weather-worn face.

There were a few sentences hastily exchanged in Hungarian and then the second sister sat down.

"Are you feeling better?" Archie asked politely, "Doctor Evans said you were unwell."

"I better than morning," the woman growled, "I Romana."

It took a second or two for the vicar to realise that the woman was offering her name, and as he sat staring at her, the twins made hand signs at each other, obviously not wanting their visitor to understand. It was at that point that Archie noticed something strange. Both women were wearing woollen mittens.

"I say, are you feeling cold?" he naiively asked, "Perhaps you're coming down with a flu bug."

Magda looked down at her hands immediately, understanding at once why the vicar had asked such a question, "No, not cold."

Archie turned to look at Romana, and caught her narrowing her eyes at her sister.

"Always we wear," she told him, "Is tradition."

The vicar had never heard of a custom that required women to wear thick mittens inside their homes and the look of disbelief on his face must have been blatantly obvious to the Getzi sisters.

"Now you go," Magda insisted, motioning at the door, "We fine, vee car."

Archie rose, not wanting to outstay his very frosty welcome, "Enjoy the pie. Good day ladies."

Romana scurried over to the table, seeing the dessert for the first time, "Ooh, look good. Bye vee car."

On the ride home, Archie's thoughts were occupied with what he had both seen and heard at the cottage. It was obvious to him that Magda Getzi was the dominant sister, she had controlled the conversation and she had been the one to tell him to leave, and Romana hadn't taken her eyes off her sister, almost waiting for instruction. Replaying the half hour inside the cottage in his mind, the vicar was sure that there were many more curious things going on inside than he had first sensed, he just needed to think through the clues. There had been a great quantity of kilner jars on the shelves to start with, but this perhaps wasn't so unusual when you considered that the women grew all of their own fruit and vegetables. The glassware was most probably used for jams and pickling. But there had been a strange smell in the room too, and not just that of the boiling stockings. It was an underlying odour of something balsam, almost like peppermint but more menthol. Perhaps the ladies were in the habit of rubbing themselves with organic potions, he wondered. All these thoughts and more besides, jiggled around in the vicar's mind as he peddled quickly towards the vicarage, and so preoccupied was he that the dreadful tea stayed inside him until the final bend when, swerving to avoid a pothole, the disgusting liquid departed Archie's stomach and hurtled upwards into his mouth. It was no use, he couldn't hold it any longer, and as a bright green car pulled up alongside, the vicar let forth and was sick up the driver's window. He recoiled in horror.

And, as if things weren't bad enough, the driver was laughing his socks off! It was Martin Fry.

Later that evening, after having managed to consume a dry piece of toast and several glasses of water, Archie phoned Doctor Evans to discuss his visit to the Getzi sisters. He confirmed all the things that the medic had told him earlier in the day, the smells, the heat, the hostile looks and the mittens. Both men were in agreement that something very odd was going on in that cottage, but neither could quite put their finger on it.

"Does it really matter?" Archie asked, starting to get impatient and tired, "Couldn't we just mind our own business and let them carry on as they are?"

"Oh yes, great idea," Doctor Evans shot back sarcastically, "Next thing one of them dies and I find myself up in court for neglect. Well done vicar!"

"Don't take the moral high ground with me," he replied stifling a yawn, "There's only one way to tackle this and it's to go up there together. We both know those women are strange, but that in itself is not illegal."

"I know, I know," said the doctor, calming down somewhat, "But I suspect that Romana Getzi might have a serious illness and as things stand she won't even so much as let me check her pulse."

"Right, if we're agreed, you can pick me up at eight in the morning. That should give us plenty of time to go up there before your morning surgery," Archie concluded.

"Don't fancy another cycle ride then, or are you SICK of them?" Dr. Evans chortled.

Archie hung up and went to bed.

Next morning, the vicar fed Hector and was just finishing his second cup of tea when the doctor arrived. It was another bright and sunny morning so, leaving in just his shirtsleeves and dog-collar, Archie locked the back door and jumped in the car. Doctor Evans looked sheepishly across at his passenger and began the process of contriving an apology.

"Look, about what I said last night old chap," he muttered, "It was only said in jest."

"News certainly travels fast," Archie replied tersely, "I suppose Martin popped straight round did he?"

"Erm, no, actually I was in The Swan when he popped in for a pint."

"Great," the vicar mumbled, sinking back in his seat, "So now the whole town knows."

Pulling up outside the stone cottage, the men could see that the curtains were already drawn and one of the sisters was busy sweeping the step. They glanced at each other before stepping out of the vehicle and tried their best to smile cheerfully.

"Hello there Ms. Getzi," the doctor called as he strode towards the old lady, "I've come to see Romana."

"Humph," the woman growled, pointing at the vicar, "Why him?"

"Reverend Matthews has come at my request," Doctor Evans started to say, but the explanation was lost on Magdalena and she just retreated into her home, dragging the broom behind her.

Both men stepped forward another pace, hoping dearly that she would leave the door open. She did.

"You want tea?" Magda Getzi asked, pointing at the kettle on the open fire, "I can make."

"No!," shot Archie, far too hastily, "I mean, no, please don't trouble yourself."

"Humph," the woman growled again, "I get Romana."

Slowly straightening up, the old Hungarian hobbled into the adjoining room and spoke in hushed tones to her sister, leaving the men to look around at the various objects in the kitchen.

"What do you think this is?" Archie whispered, sniffing at a pot of green gelatinous fluid on the table.

"Smells like eucalyptus," Dr. Evans told him, leaning over to check, "Some kind of balm I think."

The vicar looked around. He could count eight more pots of the same mixture on the shelves and numerous others containing different concoctions in various colours, "And these?"

"No idea," the doctor shrugged, "Certainly not anything I've ever prescribed."

"Humph," Magda grunted from behind them, "Romana here. She no feel better."

The other sister appeared behind her twin and frowned at the men, "What you look?"

"Ah, Romana," Doctor Evans smiled, "We were just admiring your vast collection of potions, are they home cures? Something you made yourselves perhaps?"

"I sit," Romana grumbled, eyeing him warily, "You look, I no feel good."

While the old women pottered over to their comfortable chairs either side of the roaring fire, the doctor winked at Archie and said, "Romana, may I check your pulse my dear?"

The vicar followed his companion's eyes down to the women's hands, which were once again covered in thick woollen mittens. He was intrigued as to how they could bear such heavy items in the heat of the kitchen, which even at this early hour was roasting hot.

"Pull sa," Romana repeated, her foreign accent thick and deep, "How you do?"

"Remember, I asked you yesterday," the doctor explained, "It's to see how fast your heart is beating."

He gently tugged at the cuff of the mitten, intending to uncover the old woman's slender wrist.

"No," Magdalena snapped, putting a heavy hand on the medic's arm, "I say no."

"Come along dear," Archie encouraged, "The doctor won't harm your sister, he's trying to help."

Romana looked down at her sister's strong hand, the fingers grabbing at Dr. Evans' jacket like the talons of a hawk, then she bubbled forth with a string of Hungarian, leaving the two visitors in complete confusion as to what was being communicated.

"I tell Magda you help," Romana said eventually in her pigeon English, "She not believe."

"Of course I will help," the doctor soothed, gently patting the old lady's hand, "And so will Reverend Matthews. But first I need to find out what's making you so poorly."

He looked sharply across at Magdalena, waiting for her consent, "Please?"

Magda Getzi nodded but narrowed her eyes at her sister, obviously still very unsure.

"Good, so now may I remove these mittens?" the doctor pleaded, "It will make my diagnosis easier."

Archie tensed, feeling the strain between himself, Doctor Evans and the old women.

"Okay," Romana told him, "Be careful, it no good."

"And it secret," Magdalena warned him sharply, "You no tell."

Reverend Matthews looked on from his position near the mantle-piece. Not more cloak and dagger business, he thought, every home around here seems to hide something.

At first the mittens came off, quite easily and without fuss, but underneath Romana's hands were bandaged in coarse linen and smelled heavily of the green balsam. Doctor Evans looked over at Magdalena and hesitated for a second before asking, "Are your hands the same?"

"Same," she confirmed, holding them up in the air, "We twin."

The doctor continued to unravel the cloth, slowly and carefully, winding it into a ball as he went. At last when it was all removed, he sat back, speechless and the vicar moved closer to see what he was looking at. No words could describe his feelings. It was a strange kind of curiosity mixed with fear and disbelief. Romana Getzi's fingers were scaly and amphibious, joined together by intricate webbed skin all the way down to her fingertips. Both hands were identical and also slathered in aromatic green gel.

Archie stood, unaware that he was open-mouthed and wide-eyed, taking in the old woman's hands. At least the doctor was attempting some semblance of composure but it was with great difficulty that he did so. Magda Getzi was the first to speak.

"Feet same," she pointed, indicating her sister's toes, "Me too."

"May I?" stuttered Doctor Evans, tugging at Romana's slippers, "I, I, really just need to see."

The twins nodded in unison and assisted him in exposing the old woman's bandaged ankles.

"How very extraordinary," Archie commented as they left the cottage an hour after their arrival, "Have you ever seen a case like that before?"

"Not likely," the doctor admitted, "The biggest foot complaint I've ever attended to was a bad case of bunions. It really is the strangest phenomena I've ever come across."

Archie pulled his seat-belt from its holder and stopped before fastening it completely. The doctor's hands were trembling slightly as he tried to get the key into the ignition.

"I say, are you alright?" he asked, "Shaken you up a bit has it?"

"Mmm, I think it has," Doctor Evans admitted, "Not every day you encounter something like that."

"Yes, well, we promised to keep it to ourselves and we will," Reverend Matthews reminded him, "Besides the women are physically quite healthy, apart from their webbed hands and feet and strange diet."

Despite being tempted to hospitalise the Hungarian women for scientific testing, both Doctor Evans and Reverend Matthews managed to keep their promise to the pensioners and continued their visits until the ladies could be persuaded to go about their daily chores with their hands uncovered. The medic thought that fresh air and less homeopathic attempts at a cure for their disability might help to alleviate some of the tender skin, leaving the twins free to go about their business mitten-free. The vicar, despite his attempts at trying to welcome the Hungarians into his congregation, concluded to let them worship whichever God pleased them in whichever way the duo felt fit but he never gave up hope that one day they would present themselves at his church.

It was only during a conversation with the Bishop that September, as they discussed Harvest Festival plans, that the Getzi sisters' names were mentioned.

"Do you have many needy people in the parish Archie my boy?" the Bishop enquired, "People who might benefit from a basket of groceries and some fresh vegetables?"

"As a matter of fact yes," he acknowledged, "There are a couple of old ladies living up on the moors."

"Really?" Bishop Honeywell exclaimed, "Out in that wilderness!"

"Two Hungarian sisters," the vicar explained, "Apparently they've lived up there for years."

"Interesting," the Bishop mused, hesitating, "Did Reverend Wilton-Hayes mention them in his chronicle?"

"No, he didn't actually," Archie confessed, wondering where this particular line of questioning was heading, "It was Doctor Evans that first mentioned them."

"Ah," came the voice from the other end of the line, "And what do you make of them? Are they normal?"

"I don't quite know what you mean," he faltered, feeling torn between keeping his promise and wanting to tell the whole tale to his superior and mentor.

"Any unusual physical traits?" the senior clergy pushed.

"Some…" Archie began warily, before being interrupted by Bishop Honeywell again.

"Aha! I think I have something you might need to read my boy, I'll dig it out and pop it in the post."

"Right you are," the vicar said, wondering what on earth it could be, "Thank you your Grace."

With preparations for the Harvest Festival service underway, Archie's conversation with Bishop Honeywell completely slipped his mind until several days later when a large brown envelope arrived in the mail. As was her usual habit, Mrs. Fry had picked up the delivery from the mat and set it down on the hall table, therefore it wasn't until late afternoon on his way upstairs to change that the vicar noticed its arrival.

"I recognise that shaky handwriting," Reverend Matthews said to himself as he slid a letter opener across the seal, "What have we here then?"

Inside was a newspaper cutting, dated August 3rd 1950. It was over twenty-five years old. Carefully unfolding the parchment, Archie spread it out on the walnut table and began to read:

'AFTER THREE WEEKS OF INTENSE SEARCHING BY LOCAL POLICE, THERE IS STILL NO SIGN OF THE GETZI SISTERS WHO WENT MISSING FROM THEIR CARAVAN ON JULY 15TH. DESPITE DOOR-TO-DOOR QUESTIONING AND A GROUND TEAM ON HAND, NO CLUES HAVE BEEN FOUND.

THE HUNGARIAN TWINS WERE REPORTED AB-SENT FROM A SCHEDULED PERFORMANCE BY THEIR EMPLOYER, GUSTAV LIMAN OF LIMAN'S CIRCUS FAME.

KNOWN TO THEIR FANS AS THE 'FROG SISTERS' ROMANA AND MAGDA GETZI ARE REPORTED AS HAVING UNUSUAL WEBBED FINGERS AND TOES AND SPEAKING VERY LITTLE ENGLISH.

THE CIRCUS COMMUNITY IS REPUTEDLY A TIGHT-KNIT ONE, THEREFORE INSPECTOR TRAFFORD OF C.I.D. HAS CONCLUDED THAT THERE IS NO CAUSE FOR ALARM AND THAT THE WOMEN HAVE MOST PROBABLY RETURNED TO THE COUNTRY OF THEIR BIRTH.'

Underneath the column was a black and white photograph of a much younger looking Magdalena and Romana Getzi, smiling reluctantly for the camera with their webbed digits on show.

Archie carried the newspaper cutting into the kitchen and picked up the telephone.

"Evans?" he inquired, "Can you come? There's something you need to see."

Chapter Ten

Blackie Jenkins

Two doors down from the Wheeler's, in a smart Victorian terraced house, Blackie Jenkins and his family resided in moderate comfort, through hard work, pride and love. Just like his forefathers, Blackie had worked in the coal mine all of his adult life, married a local girl with inexpensive tastes and raised his family to look out for one other and those around them. His moniker, given by old man Jenkins in jest after his son's first proper shift at the pit, was the only name by which Blackie was ever referred to. It suited him well, as every day he would go to work scrubbed as white as the sheets on his bed, but every evening he would turn up on the doorstep covered from head to toe in coal dust, as black as the ace of spades. Of course, the other mine workers also returned home covered in the minerals that they sought deep under the ground, but Blackie Jenkins always looked dirtier with the only whiteness on him being two small rings around his eyes and his pearly teeth.

Mrs. Jenkins was known as a bit of a tyrant when it came to running her household, insisting her husband undress in the back yard before entering the kitchen where he was expected to throw his overalls straight into a bucket of hot soapy water to remove the worst of the grime before they were boiled. Even the Jenkins children knew better than to leave dirty clothes in their bedrooms, and they would never dare to play outside with their friends until their homework was finished and their daily chores completed. Most of the other miners joked that his wife was the reason that Blackie did so much overtime, but he took the comments in jest and never said a negative word about her. In truth, it made him proud to know that his better half was diligent in keeping their home pristine, although a little less nagging wouldn't have gone amiss.

Blackie didn't own a car, he didn't need to. The children caught the bus to school or walked, depending on the weather, and he could walk to work within fifteen minutes of leaving home. As far as he was concerned, everything they needed was right there in town and whatever went on outside was of no interest. Naturally he read the newspapers and commented on national affairs with his friends, but the bubble that was Blackie's world was sewn up tight, just the way he liked it. He went to work, came home, ate dinner, watched television and went to bed. The routine was set and a satisfactory one it was too, continuing unchanged six days a week. However, the seventh day was different.

Instead of staying in bed on his day of rest, Blackie Jenkins rose at his usual hour leaving his wife in bed, tended to the flowers in his window boxes, polished his children's shoes ready for school the next day, waved his family off to church after cooking their breakfast and then he would don an apron and serve up the best Sunday roast in town on their return before disappearing to the pub for a couple of pints.

It was very rare that Reverend Matthews came into contact with the head of the Jenkins family. They were like passing ships in the night, one going one way in pursuit of his work and the other appearing at some totally different hour on an errand in town. It wasn't intentional, but the vicar felt that the miner was fully entitled to spend his only day off at leisure and ignored his absence at church. Therefore, it was quite to shock when Archie to found Blackie Jenkins sitting in a pew one evening quiet as a mouse. The man looked as though he was in prayer, with his shoulders hunched and head bowed, so the vicar took a wide berth and tiptoed to the altar via the east wall.

"Evening vicar," Mr. Jenkins called, "No need to be quiet on my account."

"Evening," he replied, turning to face the stranger, "I thought you might be in prayer, didn't want to disturb you. I don't believe we've met…"

"Blackie Jenkins," the miner called, getting up to shake the clergyman's hand, "I'm not what you call a regular church-goer see, but my wife comes every Sunday with the kids, Jilly Jenkins."

"Yes, indeed she does," Archie smiled, suddenly realising whom he was talking to, "I appreciated her help with the Harvest Festival last week, very kind to assist with decoration, the church looked splendid."

"She's a good 'un," Mr. Jenkins admitted, "Always thinking of others."

"Quite." The vicar nodded politely, "I've just popped in to say a few prayers of my own, please do continue." He gestured towards the pew and clasped his hands.

"Oh no," Blackie said, looking startled, "I came to think, not pray. My time for praying has long gone."

"Come now," Archie soothed, "It's never too late, Our Lord is always ready to listen if we let him."

The other man stood awkwardly thinking of something to say but nothing came, so instead he took out a large handkerchief and blew his nose which in turn caused a heavy bout of coughing.

"Are you alright Mr. Jenkins?" Reverend Matthews asked, noticing the miner's hand shaking slightly.

"Fine," Blackie laughed, "Just a bit of a cold coming."

"If you're sure, perhaps you should pop in to see Dr. Evans at his next surgery."

Mr. Jenkins shook his head, "Bloody quacks, don't know their arses from their elbows."

The vicar laughed, embarrassed at the man's crude language but not wanting to chastise him either.

"Well, I'll bid you goodnight then Mr. Jenkins. Perhaps you'll pop in again sometime?"

"Maybe," Blackie answered heading for the door, "You just never know."

After this incident Archie was curious to find out why the miner had been in the church that night. He didn't suspect it was anything dishonest but rather wondered whether the man had been in need of someone to talk to. Of course, it could always have been the rouse for an extra-marital liason, using the church as a meeting point, but he doubted it very much, Mr. Jenkins just didn't seem the type. Instead of driving himself to distraction wondering what had been going on, the vicar decided to pry gently by asking the coal-worker's wife, and what better opportunity than the following Sunday after service.

"Mrs. Jenkins," Reverend Matthews smiled, shaking Jilly's hand as she left, dressed in a smart polyester suit and striped scarf, "How's your husband?"

"My husband?" she repeated, "He's fine thank you vicar. Why do you ask?"

Archie hadn't prepared himself for the countering question and stood open-mouthed until she probed further.

"Have you seen him recently? Only I don't remember him saying he'd met you."

"No, no," Archie heard himself saying, "I just like to ask about all my parishioners."

Jilly Jenkins looked unconvinced and tipped her head on one side, "I'll tell him you asked after him vicar."

It was only later, as he stood in the vestry disrobing, that Reverend Matthews wondered if he's stirred up a barrel load of trouble. If Blackie Jenkins hadn't mentioned to his wife that he'd met the vicar, she would wonder how they'd met and why her husband hadn't said anything. Or would she? He asked himself. Maybe the female species weren't as complicated as he thought, although he didn't have much experience in how marital communications fared in situations like this. Best not to worry himself, the vicar concluded, it will all blow over but if Mr. Jenkins does happen to present himself at church again, we'll have to have a chat about the reasons for not telling his family. Perhaps the poor man's worried about something? But what?

"Egg mayonnaise or ham?" Mrs. Fry questioned, hovering at the refrigerator door.

"I really don't mind either," Archie muttered, glancing up from his crossword momentarily.

"Oh, by the way," Elizabeth continued sliding a pack of ham from the shelf, "Martin saw you going into the church late last night, couldn't you sleep?"

The vicar looked up, startled, "It certainly wasn't me, not last night. Could he have been mistaken?"

"No!" the housekeeper scoffed, "You know Martin, he might have had a few pints but he definitely saw someone. He just presumed it was you I suppose."

"How very odd," Archie mused putting down his pen, "I wonder who it was."

"Someone looking to have their sins forgiven I'll bet," Mrs. Fry chuckled as she opened the bread bin.

"Or someone up to no good," the vicar muttered.

That night, after a restless nap on the sofa and no sign of his mind winding down for the night, instead of going up to bed Archie put on his cardigan and let himself out through the back door. It seemed that Hector had ideas about joining him for a walk too, and soon man and feline were walking side by side up the driveway. The vicar wondered what anyone might think, should he have the misfortune to be seen, a lonely clergyman and his enormous black cat wandering around in the dark, but it was unlikely that there would be any visitors to the vicarage at this late hour. However, it seemed that the church was a different matter, and as Archie unlatched the gate to enter the gloomy churchyard, he caught sight of a figure entering the great arched doors. If it hadn't been for the dim light of the porch lantern, he might have believed himself mistaken, but the beam was enough to distinguish a middle-aged man in a dark jacket and cloth cap. The vicar followed, careful to turn the handle gently to avoid it creaking. Once inside he adjusted his eyes to the darkness and stood looking at the hunched figure halfway down the aisle. Within seconds a rough gasping cough identified the man as Blackie Jenkins.

"Mr. Jenkins? Is that you?" Archie called out, "Are you alright?"

"Bloody hell vicar!" the man cursed, "You gave me the fright of my life! What are you doing here?!"

"I might well ask you the same question. Nasty cough you've got there."

It didn't take long for Archie to persuade Blackie Jenkins to accompany him back to the vicarage, with the offer of a hot cup of tea and some ginger nut biscuits. Hector dutifully followed, much to Mr. Jenkins amusement.

"Your cat is he?" Blackie asked, stroking the feline's soft furry head, "He's a fair size."

"Well, he's adopted me, rather than the other way around," the vicar admitted, looking affectionately at the cat as he purred gently, "Very good company though."

"Jilly won't have any animals," the miner confessed, "Says she has enough to clean up without pet hairs."

Reverend Matthews suspected that the subject was a bone of contention between the couple.

Once inside, Archie busied himself with filling the kettle and wondered how best to get Mr. Jenkins to open up about what he'd been doing in the church so late in the evening. As it happened, Blackie was actually pondering the very same matter.

"Can I ask you something, man to man?" Blackie Jenkins finally said, not taking his eyes from Hector.

"Of course," the vicar responded, "Whatever we discuss stays right here, you know that don't you?"

"Well," Blackie hesitated, "As a man of the cloth, are you bound by law to keep people's secrets, you know, if they tell you something in confidence?"

Archie sighed, "I think you're confusing me with a Catholic priest. It's usually they who listen to confession and give advice to their parishioners."

"Oh…." Blackie trailed off, ashamed that he didn't know the difference.

"However," Archie continued, "I never divulge anything that someone has told me in private. That is simply the kind of man I am Mr. Jenkins."

He paused, hoping that the man sitting at his kitchen table would now open up. "Mr. Jenkins?"

Blackie took the cup of tea that was being offered to him and began heaping spoonful after spoonful of sugar into it, "Perhaps you'd better sit down vicar, this might take some time."

Archie pulled out a chair and opened the packet of biscuits, "I'm all ears," he said.

The next few hours found the two men deep in conversation and consuming several more cups of tea. It was midnight by the time the miner got up to leave, rubbing Hector along his back as he rose.

"You can't tell anyone," Blackie warned, "But I have a feeling I can trust you."

"You can," Archie promised, following him to the door, "I just wish I could do something to help."

Mr. Jenkins fumbled for his handkerchief, coughing loudly and momentarily losing his breath, "I'll be alright, it's the family I worry about."

The vicar patted his visitor on the back, both to help relieve the cough and to console him.

"Night vicar," Blackie managed through his wheezing, "No doubt I'll see you again soon. Thank you."

Archie nodded, "Any time."

The enormity of Blackie Jenkins' troubles had a profound effect on Reverend Matthews, causing him to sleep even less than usual and also to spend many solitary hours cooped up in his study. Given his solemn promise not to reveal the coal-miner's woes to anyone else, Archie felt as though a heavy weigh hung around his neck, causing him to plunge into a very dark mood. If only there were some way in which he could alleviate the poor man's anxiety.

Archie had always been a great confidante, the kind of person that could tolerate listening to other people's woes, as he felt quite certain that his own life contained more heartbreak and stress than any one human should be made to endure. That was, however, up until the moment that Blackie Jenkins had unloaded his heavy burden. Now it was with a benevolent mind and rational train of thought that the vicar set about finding the best course of action. Unfortunately, for them both, time was not on his side.

The vicar sat motionless, replaying the conversation with Blackie Jenkins in his mind. Over and over it went, Archie trying desperately to remember every detail, and then making notes about what needed to be done when the time came to step forward to help. It wasn't going to be easy, he knew that for a fact, but there were certain things that he needed Mr. Jenkins to do now before it was too late, and one of those things was to tell his wife exactly what was going on. The vicar knew that Blackie wouldn't be easily convinced but perhaps, with a bit of persuasion, the miner might see that he had a moral obligation to tell his lifelong partner this terrible secret. However, Archie definitely didn't want to be the one to tell her.

A few nights later, sitting in the vicarage kitchen drinking tea, the vicar and Mr. Jenkins mulled over the consequences of coming out with the truth, although they were miles apart in their thinking.

"It's certainly becoming more difficult to explain my absence," Blackie admitted, "Jilly thinks I've got another woman, I'm sure of it."

"You're going to have to come straight," Archie warned him, "It's only fair."

"Easy for you to say," the miner scoffed, "I bet you don't have money worries do you?"

"That's got nothing to do with it Blackie," he replied, consciously using the man's first name to ensure a certain degree of trust and friendship, "How much time do we have?"

"We?" Mr. Jenkins laughed, "Don't you tangle yourself up in this."

"You know what I mean," Archie sighed, getting up and opening a cupboard, "Fancy something stronger?"

He pulled out a bottle of whisky and two glasses. Blackie Jenkins just nodded.

During service the following Sunday, Reverend Matthews suddenly became aware of someone staring at him. It was an odd sensation, sending prickles shooting up the back of his neck. He scanned the crowd, naturally seeing every face looking at him, but one pair of eyes were wide and unblinking. They belonged to Jilly Jenkins. Sitting three rows back from the front, with her long hair neatly pinned into a bun, Jilly's face was almost as crimson as the blouse that she wore. Such was her demeanour that the vicar faltered in his reading and had to take a couple of seconds to gather his thoughts. It was only afterwards, as the parishioners chatted outside, that he felt the wrath of Mrs. Jenkins' tongue.

"Blackie came home drunk last Thursday night," she hissed, keeping her voice low to avoid attracting attention, "Says he was with you."

"Yes," Reverend Matthews admitted, "We did have a drink, but only a couple of whiskies. I can assure you that it wasn't enough to get him drunk."

"My husband has never touched a drop of booze in his life," Jilly went on, "Up until he met you."

Archie rolled his eyes, aware that several members of the congregation had stopped talking and were now looking their way, "Mrs. Jenkins, I had no idea. It won't happen again," he whispered feebly.

"Carol, Adam, come on, let's get back," Jilly called to her children who had wandered over to look at some ancient gravestones, "Whatever is going on vicar, I need to know," she said, lowering her voice, "For the sake of my marriage."

Archie tried his best to look sympathetic but the woman simply turned on her heel and walked off.

"Everything alright vicar?" Martin Fry queried, crunching along the gravel in his leather brogues.

Archie continued to watch Jilly Jenkins, "I'm not really sure Martin, not sure at all."

Over the next few weeks, Blackie Jenkins became a regular visitor at the vicarage. He had given up going into the church, explaining to the vicar that he'd only gone there in the beginning for peace and quiet, not for any sudden urge to pray. Besides, he was a non-believer, or at least he thought he was. One night the conversation took a deeply serious note and touched on this very subject.

"So, you reckon that we all go up to meet our maker after death," Blackie stated casually.

"That's what the Bible teaches us," Archie told him, "Do you doubt that?"

"I don't know if I believe in Heaven," the miner admitted, taking a gulp of tea, "Perhaps there's, nothing. Perhaps we just get extinguished and there's no such thing as souls."

"That's very cynical," the vicar said, choosing his words carefully, "But given the circumstances...."

"I'm not afraid," Mr. Jenkins answered, "I just want to see my family right."

Archie took a deep breath and folded his arms across his chest, "Blackie, how much have you saved?"

The coal-miner rubbed his eyes with the back of his hands, "Enough to see them through for a couple of years," he replied tearfully, "But not much longer, plus my standard pension."

"Maybe I can have a word with the Bishop," Reverend Matthews offered, "There are charities who..."

"No!" snapped Mr. Jenkins, quite adamant that this wasn't what he wanted, "All my life I've grafted. I looked after my parents when my dad couldn't work any longer, putting food on the table for six of us. What have I got to show for all those years down the mine? Nothing more than a roof over our heads! Do you know we haven't even had a holiday for over five years, vicar? I'm always down that bloody mine!"

The following day, Reverend Matthews made a resolution. He was going to convince Blackie Jenkins to come clean to his wife. The longer this went on, their nightly chats in the vicarage kitchen, going over and over the consequences of what was going to happen, the more he felt the situation getting out of control. The enormity of holding in someone else's secret was beginning to take its toll on the vicar's health too and other people had started to notice.

Elizabeth Fry had naturally been the first to show her concern, mentioning casually over morning coffee that he looked tired and withdrawn.

"And another thing," she lectured, setting up the ironing board, "I know you haven't been sleeping."

"You do?" Archie asked incredulously, "How did you come to that conclusion?"

"You didn't bring your sheets down to be washed on Monday," she huffed, wagging a finger at him, "And I know how fussy you are about having fresh bedding."

"Guilty as charged," he sighed, picking Hector up in his arms, "We've got rather a lot on our minds haven't we old chap?" He rubbed the cat affectionately under its chin and set him down on the floor again.

"Why don't you let me bring you a tonic?" Mrs. Fry offered kindly, "Just to help you sleep?"

"What's in.......?" Archie began, but then changed his mind, "Wait, I really don't want to know do I?"

Elizabeth giggled, her childish, innocent laugh that always brought a smile to her employer's face.

"I'll fetch it for you at tea-time," she promised.

That night, after drinking the peppermint concoction as directed by his housekeeper, Reverend Matthews slept soundly for a full eight hours. It was the first time in over a month that he'd been able to fall into such a deep slumber and, apart from a strange dream involving ghosts and guns, he woke feeling refreshed and positive. The most important thing that a good night's sleep had taught him was that when something was bothering you to the point of distraction, the cause of concern needed to be resolved. In this case, the problem was Blackie Jenkins and the burden of his secret. There seemed nothing else for it, without risking his own health and the concerns of the parish, Archie would have to force Mr. Jenkins to tell his wife, and very probably his employer too, what was going on. Therefore, when the miner appeared at the vicarage door that evening, Archie was more than ready for verbal combat.

"Are we agreed then?" the vicar asked his visitor, after having spoken to him for over an hour, "We'll do this together, tomorrow evening after you finish work."

Blackie Jenkins sighed and then began coughing, air rasping in his throat as he struggled to get it under control, "Alright," he managed hoarsely, "Come down to ours about seven."

"Is there anything we haven't covered?" Archie asked thoughtfully, "Anything your wife might ask?"

Mr. Jenkins shook his head, "Most of what she'll want to know is in the hospital report," he spluttered, wiping his mouth with a handkerchief, "I've got it here."

He took a slim white envelope from his jacket pocket and slid it across the table to his companion.

"Go on," Blackie urged, "Read it."

Archie slid out a double-sided letter and began to read, when he'd finished he sat back and looked closely at the man in front of him. Now he could see the changes, how in just a few weeks the miner had lost a lot of weight, his face had become pallid and the folds of skin around his neck had become loose and saggy.

"It's definitely from smoking then," he sighed, "Nothing to do with the coal dust."

"Twenty Woodbines a day for over thirty years," the other man confirmed, "Self-inflicted cancer."

The vicar turned to look out into the dark night. He never bothered to draw the curtains in the kitchen, and now the shadows from nearby trees were bobbing up and down in the wind like headless ghouls. He got up and took out a full bottle of whisky.

"Oh Blackie," he tutted, "For the sake of your family it would have been better if your illness had been caused by your job wouldn't it? At least that way Jilly could've claimed for compensation."

"Tell me about it," Mr. Jenkins remonstrated, balling his fingers up to make a fist, "Now she'll get absolutely nothing and will have to scrimp and scrape for the rest of her days."

Archie unscrewed the whisky and opened his mouth to speak.

"And don't you bloody start harping on about charity," Blackie warned, "My Jilly won't take it, too proud."

"Very well," the vicar conceded, "Let's see what happens when we break it to her tomorrow."

Blackie Jenkins got up to leave, "Alright. Better let you get some rest, you'll need it."

The next afternoon, around four o'clock, after waiting for Elizabeth to leave, Reverend Matthews put on his jacket and prepared for the walk into town. His appointment at the Jenkins' house wasn't for some time yet, but Archie had planned to run a few errands first and then, time allowing, to call in at The Swan for a pint to give him Dutch courage before facing Jilly. Just as he was about to close the back door, he caught sight of a white envelope on the table, the very same item that Blackie Jenkins had given him to read the night before. Archie slid the letter safely into his pocket and patted it. Mrs. Jenkins would need to read that, he thought, to fully understand the enormity of what they were about to tell her, that her husband of twenty-five years only had a few months to live.

It was a windy afternoon, the Autumn season now sweeping leaves off the trees and turning everything from green to golden brown, and the vicar walked briskly downhill carefully avoiding muddy tracks and puddles. Behind him the church looked grey and gloomy as it always did, and he couldn't help but think about a time in the near future when pall-bearers would carry Blackie's coffin through the doors. Such were the dreary thoughts that filled Archie's mind that afternoon as he drew closer to the houses and shops in the valley below, and it wasn't until he reached the main crossroads that the vicar became aware of the panic around him.

A siren blared in the distance, an awful droning sound, like that of the warnings in the blitz during the war. People were running, a look of fear in their eyes, legs carrying them hurriedly on, everyone running in the same direction. Archie stood, frozen to the spot and watched them go, down the main thoroughfare and on towards the coal mine. Suddenly he was joining them, a spark igniting in his brain, telling him what he feared to hear, there had been a serious accident in the pit.

Gathering at the gates alongside most of the adult townsfolk, Reverend Matthews waited for news. There seemed to be pandemonium at the pit-head, miners rushing franticly back and forth while the bosses shouted instructions. He could make out the stout figure of Ted Bennett, waving his arms and rushing to where a huge metal cage was climbing to the surface. There was a terrible rumbling under the ground and men shouted in blind panic. Archie pushed himself through crowd and leapt over the wooden fence, he needed to help, and needed to know how bad it was. Just as he reached the blackened men standing at the head of the shaft, the cage door opened and a group of dusty miners came hurtling out, gasping and spluttering, trying desperately to fill their lungs with clean air. The vicar waited with baited breath.

Mr. Wheeler was the first to speak, sitting back against a small slag heap, his hands resting on his knees, "The whole shaft collapsed," he wheezed, "One of the pillars gave way."

"Is anyone still down there?" a voice asked, full of urgency and fear.

The man nodded and took off his safety helmet, "Blackie's down there."

Archie turned to the site foreman who was hunched over next to Mr. Wheeler, "You have to get him out."

"It's too late," the miner told them, "Blackie held up the shaft so that we could all get out, pushed his back up against it he did. Just as we got in the cage we heard the explosion."

Reverend Matthews felt a lump in his throat and he willed himself not to cry, "Isn't there a chance...?"

Mr. Wheeler shook his head, "He never could have survived that," he croaked.

As Archie held Jilly Jenkins in his arms half an hour later, he breathed heavily, trying desperately to stay strong but feeling himself crack on the inside.

"I'm just going to check on the kids," Mrs. Jenkins sobbed, pulling herself away from the vicar, "Carol hasn't said a word, just locked herself in her room."

Archie watched her go, and realised that now was his chance to save Blackie's family from the hardship he'd ultimately feared. If the pit bosses didn't know about Mr. Jenkins' cancer, they would pay his widow out in full, believing that a life had been lost due to negligence and safety issues in the mine.

He opened the Rayburn door and watched the embers glowing inside then, carefully taking the hospital report from his jacket, Archie threw it inside, making sure that every scrap of evidence burned down to a cinder. He finished his task just as Jilly Jenkins returned to the kitchen.

"So,," she sniffed, dabbing at her eyes, "Are you going to tell me what Blackie was up to? After all he can't tell me himself now can he."

Archie shrugged, "Nothing at all to worry about, just a bit of insomnia. We were two sleepless souls, chatting away about everyday things," he lied, trying to sound sincere.

Jilly sighed, "I knew he was a good man. My Blackie was the best."

Chapter Eleven

Peter & Valerie Gould

Bang! Bang!

There it was again, the familiar shooting sound that woke Reverend Matthews from his slumber at least four times a week. This time it was later than usual, around half past five in the morning and, instead of trying to get back to sleep, he dressed and walked into town to see if Florence Wheeler needed a hand with her deliveries. The vicar hadn't been to help the little woman much during the summer months, as he'd been busy with parish business and then lately with Blackie Jenkins, firstly helping the poor man to face his incurable illness and then afterwards consoling Jilly as she came to terms with her husband's death. Now, as he strode purposely towards the terraced cottages, Archie reflected upon the past ten months, the duration of his post as vicar in this place with its quirky townsfolk. He'd certainly heard his fair share of secrets since moving here, that was for sure, but nothing that disturbed him enough to make him want to relocate. As he knocked on the Wheeler's door, Archie wondered if he would ever settle.

"Oh, what a surprise," Florence grinned, "I wasn't expecting you vicar!"

"I was up early Mrs. Wheeler, so thought you might appreciate a hand," the vicar confessed.

"That would be grand," the little woman smiled, retreating back down the hallway, "I'll just get the baskets from the kitchen."

A couple of minutes later, with a basket on each arm, Reverend Matthews walked side by side chatting to Florence Wheeler about her daily life and the goings on in the town.

"We've still not got over that terrible explosion at the mine," she told him, shaking her head slowly, "Poor Blackie, he was in the prime of his life too."

The vicar nodded, showing that he understood the grief that had swept this neighbourhood, "A good man, I only really got to know him a couple of months ago."

"Didn't believe in going to church, or God for that matter," the woman chirped, "Still, takes all sorts."

"Where are we off to first?" Archie asked, trying to steer the conversation to something more cheerful.

Mrs. Wheeler took a list from her cardigan pocket and unfolded it, "Let me see….Oh yes, a loaf and a plum crumble for Valerie Gould. Just given birth to her sixth child she has, a year between each one! They breed like rabbits those two, Pete needs to learn to keep it in his trousers, or buy a television set!"

The vicar stifled a laugh, Florrie Wheeler certainly didn't hold back with her opinions but her dry humour was a good tonic at that hour in the morning.

"Six children," he repeated, "My goodness, she must have her hands full. I don't seem to remember Mrs. Gould, or her husband for that matter…"

"She comes to church about once every couple of months," Florence told him, "When her mother comes over to stay, she's too busy running after her little ones the rest of the time."

"Yes quite," Archie answered, wondering what kind of chaos the Gould home must be in with half a dozen infants under the age of seven, "And Mr. Gould, what does he do?"

"He owns the chip shop on Lower Street," came the response, "You must have been there."

The vicar thought for a second, "Do you know, I honestly can't remember the last time I had a battered cod, certainly not since I moved here."

"That'll be Elizabeth Fry spoiling you with her pies and beef stews," Mrs. Wheeler chuckled, "But seriously you should try Pete's fish and chips, they're the best for miles."

They walked on a short distance before stopping to make their first delivery, "I won't be long," Florence told Archie, taking a dish and a loaf from one of the baskets, "And thank you vicar."

Returning to the vicarage some time later, Reverend Matthews arrived just as his housekeeper was letting herself in through the back door. She didn't seem surprised to see him out and about so early and simply wandered over to the kettle to start making a brew.

"Elizabeth?" the vicar ventured, still thinking about Pete and Valerie Gould.

"Mmm?" she mumbled, busying herself with the teapot and cups.

"Do you and Martin ever have fish and chips?"

Mrs. Fry let out a loud laugh and turned around, "What kind of a question is that? Of course we do, every Friday night, it's a tradition in our house."

"Oh, I see," Archie replied, a little red-faced, "I didn't realise. I shall have to treat myself one evening."

It wasn't until the following Saturday, with Elizabeth taking her regular half day off to visit her sister that the vicar was left to fend for himself in the kitchen. Of course, there were plenty of fillings and bread to make a sandwich but, now that the cold weather was starting to arrive, something warm and substantial was required. It was then, sitting in his study with his coffee long gone cold, that Archie thought about venturing into town to buy a fish supper. He didn't exactly relish the idea of walking into town on a cold, foggy afternoon, but gazing down at Hector who lay belly up in front of the fire, the vicar braced himself. That lazy cat would enjoy the cod just as much as me, he thought wistfully.

It was five o'clock by the time Reverend Matthews arrived in Lower Street and a queue of customers were lined up outside the take away waiting to be served. He sniffed the air in anticipation and his stomach gave a loud rumble. The vicar wound his scarf a little tighter and joined the line behind Bill Wheatley, who delighted in regaling the new arrival with tales of his racing pigeons. Archie smiled now and again, making the right noises to convince Bill that he was listening, until the queue started to shorten and he was able to step through the shop doorway. He was immediately hit by a wave of warm air, the sizzling sound of the fryers and the mouth-watering aroma of fried food. The vicar shuffled forwards behind Mr. Wheatley and looked at the food on offer inside the heated glass cabinets. Saveloy sausages, meat pies, fishcakes, potato scallops and fish, lots and lots of crispy battered fish.

"Hello vicar," a cheerful male voice boomed over the noise of the fryers, "What can I get you?"

Archie touched his dog-collar absent-mindedly, he'd put it on without thinking this morning, people must think he never switched from being clergy to normal man.

"Good afternoon," he replied, looking thoughtfully at the choices on the large plastic board high up behind the counter, and then looking down at the server, "I think I'll have cod and chips please."

"Ah, right," mumbled Peter Gould, for it was the owner who was taking care of the vicar's order, "Can you hang on a few minutes while I batter and fry a fresh one for you?"

"Oh no need," Archie insisted, pointing at the fish on display, "One of those will be fine."

"If it's all the same to you, I'll do it fresh for you, won't take long," and before the vicar could reply, the hefty bulk of Peter Gould had shifted away from the counter and was waddling towards the chiller.

The vicar looked around. People were gazing at him, wondering why he'd caused a delay. He blushed.

It took much longer than anticipated for the chip shop owner to prepare Reverend Matthews' food, but luckily most people seemed happy to be given the fish that lay already battered in the heated unit. It seemed unnecessary of Mr. Gould to have gone to so much trouble just for the vicar some whispered, but most customers were oblivious to the fuss, simply wondering if the clergyman ate a special diet. Finally the cod and chips was ready, salted well, doused in vinegar and wrapped up tightly in yesterday's news.

Archie counted out the correct money and lifted his package from the counter, "Thank you very much."

"You're very welcome vicar," Peter Gould grinned, gathering up the coins with his chunky fingers, "Hope to see you again. Have a pleasant evening."

Back home, with an empty plate and a very satisfied cat, Archie lifted a mug of tea to his lips. That was quite possibly the best fish and chips I've ever eaten, he mused, blowing the steaming liquid gently, no wonder Peter Gould's shop is so popular. Hector lay back on the sofa at his human's side and began to wash his face with a large furry paw, feline instinct telling him that his whiskers might need cleaning after eating half a portion of cod fillet. The vicar stroked the cat gently on his head, this was the life.

"Did you try the chip shop?" Mrs. Fry inquired the following day after church, as she and Martin left.

"Yes, actually I did," Archie admitted, "And rather good it was too."

"Hope you didn't share it with that fat cat," Martin joked, jiggling his car keys, "Pete's fish is tasty."

The vicar nodded and then said thoughtfully, "I must say I was rather surprised that he went to the trouble of cooking me a fresh piece, when the chip shop was so busy."

"Oh, had he sold out?" Elizabeth queried, not quite realising what he meant.

"No, no, there were fish ready but he still insisted on doing a fresh one just for me."

Martin winked at his wife and nudged her elbow, "Special V.I.P. treatment eh?"

Archie laughed nervously, embarrassed that he'd mentioned it now but the couple were already putting on their coats and getting ready to leave, unaware of the vicar's rosy cheeks.

It was now late in November and time for Bishop Honeywell to pay his pre-Christmas visit to the parish. Reverend Matthews was looking forward to having some company at the vicarage and, as usual, Elizabeth Fry had been cooking a wide selection of treats in anticipation of the old man's visit. The Aga was stoked to keep the central heating running and fires were lit in the study and sitting room, ensuring the vicar's home felt warm and inviting. As Martin's Ford Cortina arrived, carrying the Bishop and his luggage, Archie drew back the bolt on the front door and welcomed his visitor inside.

"Look at you my boy!" Bishop Honeywell exclaimed, putting his hands on the younger man's shoulders, "The healthiest I've seen you in a long while Archibald."

"That'll be my darling wife's cooking," Martin Fry interrupted, bringing a heavy brown suitcase inside.

"Indeed," Archie admitted, "Mrs. Fry certainly looks after me."

"Well, let us catch up over a pot of tea," the Bishop enthused, "But first I must go and see Elizabeth."

Reverend Matthews watched the old man scurrying down the hall towards the kitchen, instinctively knowing that his housekeeper would already be filling the kettle and setting out cake, and he couldn't help but wonder what the strong bond was between those two, a most unlikely pair of best friends.

At four o'clock, as the two clergymen sat chatting by the sitting-room hearth, Mrs. Fry appeared at the door, her duffle coat fastened, ready to leave.

"Martin and I are fetching fish and chips for our supper, would you like some?" she offered.

The Bishop looked at Archie in anticipation, "Sounds like a good idea, doesn't it?

Archie reached in his pocket for a five pound note, knowing that it would never occur to his mentor to offer to pay, "Here you go Elizabeth, and thank you."

"No, our treat, we insist," she grinned, "See you about half past five."

Bishop Honeywell clicked his tongue on his teeth, "She's very fond of you, you know."

"Well, I…" the vicar faltered, "I, must say I've grown very fond of her too."

"Just don't step over the line, my boy. Elizabeth Fry is a very complicated woman."

As Archie stood alone in the kitchen, setting out plates and cutlery, and buttering bread, he wondered what on earth his Grace had meant about Elizabeth being complicated. He sincerely hoped that the old man wasn't suggesting their relationship to be anything more than platonic, he'd be mortified if anyone, let alone the Bishop, could ever think such a thing. But, as he replayed the words in his mind, the door opened and Martin Fry came in with their fish supper.

"Here you go, enjoy," he grinned, dashing back out as fast as he'd arrived, "Elizabeth's gone to put ours on the table, just in time for 'Z Cars'."

The vicar shouted thanks to the retreating figure and went to fetch the Bishop, all worrisome thoughts about his friendship with the housekeeper temporarily vanishing.

"Have you used that fish and chip shop before?" Bishop Honeywell asked, poking at the batter with his fork and frowning slightly.

"Yes, once," Archie told him, bending to sniff at his own piece of fish, "But I have to admit, the cod I had last time didn't taste like this. A bit earthy isn't it?"

"Mmm," his companion muttered, now using his fingers to pull at something, "Seems very boney too."

"I'm so sorry, I do apologise Your Grace."

"Hardly your fault my boy," the Bishop tutted, pushing his plate away, "Perhaps we should have a slice of Elizabeth's Dundee cake instead, eh?"

Reverend Matthews cleared the crockery, scraping some of the fish into Hector's bowl but the cat simply sniffed at it disgusted and walked off.

"Dear me, that's not a good sign," the old man joked, "Must have been off."

Archie looked dismayed, he didn't like to think of the Bishop going to bed hungry, "Can I get you something else? I can manage an omelette if you fancy one?"

Bishop Honeywell laughed and patted the seat beside him, "A slice of cake will be fine, then come and tell me all about your congregation and the secrets that they hold."

Archie dutifully obliged and, trying not to miss out anything, the pair talked until well into the night.

"Elizabeth was your fish alright?" Reverend Matthews quizzed his housekeeper the next morning.

"Yes, no different to usual, why?" she confirmed, looking up from the socks she was darning.

"Ours tasted a bit, well, earthy," he confessed, "Not at all like the previous cod I've had from there."

The woman shook her head, "That's odd, never heard anyone complain about Pete's fish before."

"Bishop Honeywell agreed with me," the vicar pushed, looking for affirmation that it wasn't just his taste buds in question.

The old man looked up from his crossword puzzle, "Very boney too," he snorted.

Elizabeth rolled her shoulders and stretched, "That's not like Pete Gould's standards at all."

As the week rolled on, Reverend Matthews found himself inundated with phone calls and notes, either asking what festivities were planned for Christmas or if their child could take part in the nativity play. He dutifully answered each request with the promise that a meeting to decide the Church's celebrations would be held the following Saturday evening at the vicarage. It fascinated the vicar how people got so excited about the upcoming events still weeks away, but Elizabeth, Florence and the other townswomen had already been hard at work making plans and recruiting volunteers ensuring that the clergyman's responsibilities were well within his capabilities.

Bishop Honeywell had decided to stay on for a while. Archie didn't know whether it was to avoid the burden of loneliness over the winter months or simply because he enjoyed Mrs. Fry's cooking and the younger man's company, but he was glad of the assistance that the old man offered. Most days the Bishop could be found sitting by the fireside in the study, reading either Dickens or Wilde, but as soon as the teapot was filled or the rustle of a packet of biscuits could be detected, out he would come in search of refreshments. The vicar noticed how Elizabeth had changed her regular cooking to accommodate the elder clergyman's palate too, exchanging heavy stews and meat pies for softer meals such as quiches or poached fish, knowing that the Bishop's dentures could better handle them. These subtle changes further enforced Archie's belief that the pair had a very strong bond, something that went beyond friendship. He could never imagination anything untoward between the two, that would be absurd, but the way in which Elizabeth touched the Bishop's arm when they spoke, and the hushed voices when they were alone together caused him deep concern, something wasn't right but he had no idea what.

Saturday came around and Reverend Matthews suddenly found himself descended upon by a rowdy group of women, all with contradicting ideas and all vying for his attention. He felt uncomfortable and hot, despite being in his own home, but as he searched the room for support, a loud clap of hands brought the crowd to order.

"Ladies, ladies, please," Bishop Honeywell called, "There's plenty of time for you all to put your tuppence worth in, so let's start off by having a glass of sherry and toasting the birth of Christ."

There was a murmur amongst the group as they reached for the tiny glasses being handed around by Mrs. Fry and suddenly everything seemed calm.

The vicar sipped his tipple and looked at the Bishop who winked back, "Don't you worry about this Archibald," the elderly man whispered cheekily, "I've got it all under control."

And so the meeting progressed, with tasks delegated, lists made and notes taken, all under the watchful organisation of the Bishop, and when it finally came to a close two hours later, Archie sat back stunned. His mentor had conducted the impossible, a schedule of services and activities to suit all ages with the total agreement of the committee. Looking down at his own list, he realised that he was left with the Church services and carol singing to instigate, the things that a vicar should be allowed to concentrate on. Archie thanked the Bishop profusely and ushered the last of the cackling women out through the door.

"I am so grateful," he repeated, "Initially I was dreading that."

"Mmm, I thought so," Bishop Honeywell smirked, "Your last parish wasn't large enough to have festivities on this scale was it my boy?"

"Just the services really," Archie told him, "And a bit of holly to decorate the Church."

"Well, this year you're going to feel the love and warmth of your congregation," the old man smiled, "A fitting reward for all your hard work, don't you think?"

"Well, I've certainly tried my best to fit in," the vicar admitted shyly, "But there's still a long way to go."

"You'll get there," the Bishop promised, shifting the cushions behind his back to a more comfortable position, "I can feel a change in you Archibald, a softer side coming through."

Reverend Matthews blushed, "Oh , I don't know about that your Grace…"

"Now," his mentor interrupted, "Go and fetch us a fish supper, perhaps it will be better this time."

As Archie approached Peter Gould's shop, he could see that the door was shut and there were no customers inside. The lights were still on however and, as he peered through the wide glass pane, movement could be detected inside. Archie pushed at the door but it didn't budge. A notice inside showed the closing time as nine and as the vicar looked at his watch it clearly showed ten minutes past. A bulky figure in a white overcoat was now ambling towards him, it was the owner.

"Sorry vicar," Pete muttered, opening the door, "We close at nine, was it a supper you were after?"

Reverend Matthews nodded, "Yes, but never mind. Is there anywhere else open?"

"Come on," Mr. Gould offered, "It won't take a minute to knock the fryer back on," and with that he shuffled back behind the counter, leaving the vicar to close the door behind him.

"Really I don't want to put you to any trouble," he said, beginning to feel flustered.

"Nonsense, I've only just this minute locked up," Peter grinned, "Valerie would have my guts for garters if she knew I'd refused to serve a man of the cloth! Now then, what do you fancy, a pie maybe?"

Archie glanced at the heated cabinet in front of him. A very large piece of battered fish lay inside, crispy and golden and more than enough to share with the Bishop.

"If that's still hot, I'll have cod and chips," he said pointing to the glass display.

Peter Gould stopped turning the knobs on the fryer and looked up, a very pained expression on his face.

"Now you did say cod," he verified, furrowing his brows, "That fish there isn't cod, if I'm truthful."

"Oh, I see," the vicar responded slowly, a little confused, "I just presumed that you sold cod and chips."

"Well…" Pete confessed, "Technically we advertise fish and chips on the board, not specifically cod."

"So what type of fish is it?" Archie pressed, expecting the reply to be haddock, plaice or even hake.

"It's pike," the chip shop owner huffed, breathing through his nostrils.

"Pike! Good grief man, you can't sell pike!"

Peter Gould slammed his hands on the counter, his face turning red, "I can sell what I damn well like vicar, it's as good a fish as any and nobody complains."

Archie stepped back, creating a wider space between himself and the fuming man who eyed him angrily and a momentary thought crossed his mind. The last time he'd had fish and chips from here it had tasted earthy, and the Bishop had complained of finding bones.

"Look," he said, trying to appease the shopkeeper, "I'm sure that pike is a perfectly good fish, but to sell it battered, in a fish and chip shop, well, I'm sorry Mr. Gould but it's just not ethical."

Pete shook his head, "You just don't get it do you? Cod costs a bloody fortune, folks around here wouldn't pay the price and I've got another six young ones to feed, let alone me and my wife."

"What about trading standards?" Archie asked calmly, seeing that the man's colour had faded slightly, "There must be some kind of regulations that you should follow."

And so the conversation continued, with Reverend Matthews trying to get Peter Gould to see the moral implications of what he was doing, and the chip shop owner pressing the financial ones upon the vicar. After five minutes of bickering, both men had wearied enough to call a truce.

"I tell you what," Pete offered, pointing at the advertisement board, "If I put 'locally caught fish' on the sign, will you let the matter lie?"

"Locally caught?" Archie spluttered, "We're over twenty miles from a river."

"Please," the heavier man pleaded, "I can't afford to lose any trade. And I have got a few pieces of cod in the chiller if anyone asks, that's what I cooked for you a few weeks ago."

The vicar thought back to the delicious first fish supper he'd shared with Hector and caved in slightly. "Alright, but if anyone asks what kind of fish it is you must tell them," he insisted.

Peter wiped a speck of salt off the counter and looked up, "Deal. Now cod and chips was it?"

"You know Mr. Gould, I'm really not hungry any more, good night."

Reverend Matthews pulled the door wide and let himself out into the frosty winter night. That was the first proper confrontation that he'd had with a parishioner since he'd arrived in town and he felt distraught at how something as trivial as a fish could rile him so much. He stopped at the corner of the street and looked around, everyone was either tucked away in their cosy homes or enjoying an evening at the pub with their friends. And where was he? Out in the freezing cold, searching for supper for his eighty year old companion and he'd even failed at that. What the hell am I doing with my life? the vicar asked himself.

As he slid back in through the back door of the vicarage, Archie realised the truth behind his frustration. It wasn't his lifestyle or the mundane ritual of performing his parochial duties, it was Elizabeth. The feelings that he'd pent up inside were wrong, a man of the church should surely be able to suppress such urges he chided himself angrily, but he just couldn't help himself, she was there every day, pandering to his needs and doing so with such elegance and joy. Elizabeth Fry, married and yet so delectable.

"No joy?" Bishop Honeywell inquired, gliding into the kitchen in his long tartan dressing-gown.

"It was closed," Reverend Matthews answered quickly, "I'll make us something on toast."

The old man shuffled across the linoleum floor, his slippers making a clicking sound as he did so, coming to rest at Archie's side, his hands pressed firmly into deep pockets.

"What is it dear boy?" he questioned, "I fear you're carrying a great burden on your shoulders."

The vicar tensed, not knowing what to say but, feeling the need to reply he bowed his head and muttered, "I'm afraid that I have inappropriate feelings for someone."

"She has that effect on men," the Bishop acknowledged, "We are talking about Elizabeth aren't we?"

Archie shot his head up, meeting Bishop Honeywell's glare, "How do you know?"

"Oh, you're not the first man to be bewitched by her charms, Reverend Wilton-Hayes died of a broken heart because he couldn't have her and then of course there was her secret."

"Your Grace," Archie snapped, fired up and emotional, "I don't think I want to know."

"No, of course you don't dear boy, and that's probably the best way."

Reverend Matthews crossed to the sink and poured himself a glass of water, he felt drained and his throat was so dry that his voice croaked when he finally spoke again.

"It's not in the chronicle, he muttered, "Elizabeth's secret, I mean."

"Are you sure?!" the Bishop retorted, his features showing genuine surprise, "I need to check."

Archie watched the old man scurry down the hallway to the study and waited half an hour before following. He wasn't too concerned as he knew the real hiding place of his housekeeper's mystery.

Bishop Honeywell slid the thick black chronicle back into its resting place on the top shelf and rubbed his bushy eyebrows. He looked worried.

"Everything alright Your Grace?" Archie queried, coming into the room and closing the door.

"No, not at all," the elder man scoffed, "Quite the opposite in fact. Rather wondering why the Reverend Wilton-Hayes didn't mention anything about her."

Archie pushed his chair back a fraction and opened a drawer, "What about this?"

The Bishop eyed the brown envelope that his prodigy clutched tightly, "Is that what I think it is?"

The vicar affirmed that it was, "The final part of the puzzle if you like. Elizabeth's secret."

The old man took out a handkerchief and mopped at his brow before sinking into an armchair.

"You know, you could always destroy it without looking old boy," he whispered, "For her sake."

Archie slipped the document back into the drawer and turned the key, "It's quite safe there for now."

"If you do read it……" Bishop Honeywell began, his breath quickening.

"I only found it this morning," the vicar sighed, "And IF I read it, you'll be the first to know."

Bishop Honeywell snorted, "She's a good woman, nobody better to look after you here, why ruin what you already have?"

"It can't be that bad, surely," Archie countered, watching the old man flinch. And then a sudden realisation hit him, "Good heavens, you already know don't you?"

The Bishop swallowed, making a loud gulping sound and tilted his head back against the top of the chair, his face looking grey and years older than it had a few minutes ago.

"How could I know Archibald?" he groaned, "No more than a suspicion, that's all."

"And the envelope?" Archie pushed, needing more information, "Who hid that in the desk?"

Bishop Honeywell shook his head, "I knew Reverend Wilton-Hayes had put it somewhere but I'd hoped to find it before you did. Archibald I beseech you, please destroy it.

The vicar shook his head. "Not yet, we'll talk more in the morning Your Grace."

Chapter Twelve

Elizabeth Fry

"Archiieeeeeeee!!!" Elizabeth screamed, "Come quickly."

As soon as he heard the high pitched voice calling, Reverend Matthews stopped buttoning up his shirt and raced down the stairs two steps at a time. He knew it was a few minutes after nine, so the housekeeper could only just have arrived, a bit too soon to be reprimanding him for not washing up the supper plates. The vicar skated across the hallway, his socks failing to give any grip on the polished surface and headed towards the kitchen. No matter what he thought the problem, in no way was Archie prepared for the scene before him. Mrs. Fry was stooped over the prostrate body of Bishop Honeywell, stroking the old man's brow and whispering to him.

"Oh, thank goodness," she simpered, "I think he's had a stroke."

"Have you called an ambulance?" Archie demanded, bending down to assist.

"Yes, of course," Elizabeth cried, "It should be here soon, poor man, I wonder how long he's been lying here alone." She glanced up at the vicar, expecting an answer but Archie didn't know.

After last night's heated conversation the Bishop had gone up to bed, leaving the vicar to demolish half a bottle of scotch before turning in, hence him rising so late this morning.

"I can hear a siren," he said, standing to peer out of the window, "Let me get the door open."

Both Archie and Elizabeth rode in the back of the ambulance with the Bishop. Thankfully he was conscious but a palsy had affected one side of his face and the senior citizen was unable to speak. As he lay on the trolley, assisted by a paramedic, the old man looked slowly across at the vicar with tears in his eyes.

"You'll be fine," Reverend Matthews mouthed, not believing his own words given the man's age and declining health, "We're here. Elizabeth and I will stay with you."

"Could you sit back and fasten your seatbelt please vicar," the medical assistant asked kindly, "It'll be a bumpy road to the hospital from here."

Elizabeth tucked her hand into the crook of Archie's elbow and sobbed, a large tear rolling down her perfectly applied foundation, "Perhaps we should say a prayer," she whispered.

As he sat by the side of the Bishop's bed, watching his mentor sleep, Reverend Matthews reflected upon the previous night's dialogue and wondered if it had contributed in any way to the stroke. He knew that stress was a possible factor and blamed himself for pushing Bishop Honeywell for answers. Absentmindedly, Archie put his hand up to his breast pocket where the envelope containing Elizabeth Fry's secret now lay. He hadn't wanted to leave it in the desk, fearing that the old man might destroy it and then Archie would never know what lay inside. He glanced at the bed in dismay.

"I'm so sorry Your Grace," he uttered in hushed tones, "This is my fault."

"Why is this your fault?" Elizabeth demanded, coming into the room with two plastic cups of coffee, her face softening at the vicar's obvious distress, "You can't possibly be to blame."

Archie thought quickly, a lie springing easily to his lips, "Letting him take so much responsibility with the Christmas arrangements. It must have been too much for him."

"Nonsense," the housekeeper countered, passing one of the cups to him, and then sitting down on the opposite side of the Bishop's bed, "I haven't seen him looking so happy in a long time."

The vicar wasn't convinced but remained silent, instead focusing on the hot drink in his hand.

Sadly Bishop Honeywell never regained the ability to speak but he did manage to communicate with his visitors by notepad and pen, distributing a list of books that he wanted brought to him in hospital and writing questions for Reverend Matthews to answer during his time by the bedside. Elizabeth had efficiently drawn up a rotating shift pattern to ensure that the Bishop was visited each afternoon and evening, and Archie found himself alone in the vicarage more often as Mrs. Fry took the alternate visits to his own. He didn't mind, in fact time apart gave him a new perspective on his feelings towards her and it became easier to accept that his momentary lapse had been both immoral and unreciprocated.

During his visits to the hospital, it was almost as if the Bishop had completely forgotten about the envelope which had previously caused so much concern. Either he had no memory of the incident in the study or he'd chosen to forget, brushing the matter from his mind in one sweep. Reverend Matthews was glad in many ways, not least of all that Bishop Honeywell seemed to have dismissed Archie's admission concerning his feelings for Elizabeth Fry and gave no hint that he'd remembered the younger man's confession. At least now there would be no possibility of the housekeeper finding out how he really felt about her, which in itself might have caused him to resign from his position in the Church.

A few weeks passed and Christmas drew closer. The town became a hive of activity, with bright lights being switched on in the streets, window displays being decorated with fake snow from spray cans and above all chatter. It wasn't the usual rumble of voices in conversation, but a cheerful, jolly chatter, of people making plans, getting excited and rushing around in anticipation of their family gatherings on Christmas Day.

Reverend Matthews had dragged an old Christmas tree out of the attic and dusted off the dozens of baubles that accompanied it, hoping to brighten up the vicarage hallway with festive cheer to all who entered. However, despite the bustle of preparations and the constant stream of visitors in December, he missed the companionship of having Bishop Honeywell there to share the celebrations. The doctors had promised that if the Bishop's improvement were significant enough, they would entrust him into the vicar's care for a few days, on the premise that he would do nothing strenuous and get plenty of rest. However, three days before Christmas all that changed.

It was four o'clock and the vicar sat reading through his Christmas Eve sermon when it suddenly dawned on him that he'd left his personal hymn book in the vestry some days before. With this being such an important service, he wanted everything organised with precision and he needed to give the chosen hymns to Elizabeth the following day in order for her to have ample time to practice on the Church organ. Therefore, shrugging on his overcoat, Reverend Matthews strode down the drive, through the gate that connected to the graveyard and let himself into the cold and silent Church. He didn't plan to hang around, it was far too cold a night for that and snow had started to fall outside, so he headed straight for the vestry to collect his hymn book.

It was dark inside, with just a single dim light bulb dangling limply from the ceiling and it took Archie a few minutes to locate what he had come in search of. As he lifted the book, and turned to leave in the shadows, the vicar accidentally knocked the coat stand to the floor with a loud crash. It was heavy and cumbersome but only held his one good jacket, so within seconds Archie had managed to pull the stand upright again. It was only as he slid it back into position next to the door that he realised something had fallen out of the jacket pocket. He bent to pick it up between his fingers and immediately felt a tightening in his stomach. It was Elizabeth's secret concealed in a plain brown envelope, nothing but her name scrawled on the front in Reverend Wilton-Hayes' almost illegible handwriting. Archie pulled open the vestry door and took a sharp intake of breath. He could either light a candle and burn it right now or he could sit down, read it and face the consequences. The vicar sat down and tore the envelope open.

Shocked and repulsed, Reverend Matthews closed his eyes, trying desperately to block out the world. The vicar was vaguely aware that his hands were shaking but they did so of their own accord and he made no attempt to get them under control. A part of him was angry, mad at himself and even more so at the Bishop, but for the most part he felt an obsessive compulsive need to rid himself of everything connected to Elizabeth Fry, every shirt that she had touched and every sock darned. She had touched him too, the odd pat on the arm, rub of the shoulders or ruffle of his hair, teasingly joking with him as she did so. Perhaps the signs were there all along, Archie thought, the playful glint in her eye that he had innocently mistaken for friendliness, her blouses being just a little too see-through sometimes with delicate lace underwear peeking through where the button-holes tightened across her chest and that seductive way in which she tossed her hair up over the collar of her coat. These were real clues, he thought, not a figment of his imagination, signs that had been there all along. Elizabeth Fry, wife, housekeeper, friend and brothel keeper.

By Christmas Eve the tension at the vicarage had become so precarious that the vicar could no longer stand to be in the same room as Mrs. Fry. If she entered, he left. If she made him a drink or something to eat, he would leave it to go cold and prepare himself a meal after she'd gone home. When he did need to communicate or happened to find himself cornered by the housekeeper, Archie would feign a cold and bring a handkerchief to his face to hide his embarrassment. Elizabeth however was very astute and her woman's intuition told her to confront him.

"Out with it," she demanded, bursting into the vicar's study as he sat writing a letter that afternoon, "I want to know what's going on."

"I don't know what you mean Mrs. Fry," he fibbed, continuing to look at the blue notepaper.

"Really?" she tutted, closing the door, "I never thought I'd see the day you told a bare-faced lie."

Archie felt his ears reddening and the prickly heat sensation soon spread to his cheeks. He put the top on his fountain pen and looked up at the irate woman in front of him. Elizabeth looked even more radiant than ever, her face alight with anger and determination. They locked eyes, neither looking away until the vicar finally pulled open a drawer and took out the dreaded brown envelope. He tossed it across the desk and pointed at it, still not taking his eyes away from Elizabeth, "See for yourself," he smirked, "Reverend Wilton-Hayes kindly left me a letter filling in the blanks of your very colourful past Mrs. Fry. I wonder, does your husband know that you were once the town's most notorious madame?"

Suddenly the doorbell rang and Elizabeth, unshaken and demure, left the room to answer it. The vicar followed, determined to get rid of the visitor and have this out with his housekeeper once and for all. He'd worked himself up into a frenzy now and cursed as he padded down the hallway.

Harlot, working for a man of God. Filthy slut, sitting in Church, playing hymns on that organ! How dare she!

He followed Mrs. Fry's retreating figure to the door, taking in her tight-fitting trousers and chiffon blouse until he could walk no further and the great door was opened.

Bishop Honeywell stood smiling at his friends, assisted by an ambulance driver who supported the old man's arm with one hand and held his suitcase firmly in the other.

"Did you forget that the Bishop was coming out today?" the young medical officer asked, looking back and forth at the two stunned faces in the vicarage doorway, "Only until Boxing Day though, I'll be back to pick him up sometime in the afternoon. Is everything alright vicar?"

Reverend Matthews lurched forward and took Bishop Honeywell's arm, leaving the younger man to bring the luggage into the hallway, "Yes, yes of course," he mumbled.

The Bishop shuffled forward, making very slow progress and sounding breathless until they reached the sitting room where he visibly glowed at the sight of the fire blazing in the hearth.

Elizabeth moved around to the back of the sofa, plumping cushions and helping the old man to sit, all the time glaring at Archie over the top of the Bishop's head.

"In the kitchen now," she seethed, gritting her teeth, and then to the Bishop, "Tea?"

Bishop Honeywell nodded as best as he could and the side of his face that had escaped paralysis gave a half smile in recognition of his caring and dear friend Elizabeth.

Archie squeezed his mentor's good hand and lifted a finger, "Back in one minute."

Trying desperately to keep his thoughts in check, the vicar followed his housekeeper to the back of the house, dreading more confrontation but knowing it was inevitable.

"What the hell is your problem?" Elizabeth asked arrogantly, raising her eyebrows and waiting calmly.

"My problem?" Archie repeated, "I unknowingly have a prostitute working in my home, someone who has undoubtedly lived upon immoral earnings, and you want to know what my problem is!

The housekeeper laughed, showing perfect white teeth and perfectly painted lips.

"It was over twenty years ago," she scoffed, "Times were different after the war, people made a living by doing what they had to. The woman I was then is not the woman I am now."

"And you had no qualms about keeping it from me," the vicar continued, "Or Bishop Honeywell."

Elizabeth rubbed her cheek and hesitated, "I didn't think you needed to know, besides…."

Suddenly it dawned on him. The Bishop had known all along!

"He knew didn't he?!" Archie yelled, unable to keep his voice calm, "Bishop Honeywell knew."

"Well, yes," the woman admitted, slumping down onto a kitchen chair, "Of course he knew."

"And he, he allows the Church to pay your wages!"

"Well, no," Elizabeth corrected, "That's not strictly true. It was agreed that I would only receive a token payment from the parish funds, the Bishop pays me the rest for services rendered."

Archie rolled his eyes in disbelief.

"Look, let's just try to get through the next few days for the Bishop's sake," Mrs. Fry hissed, leaning across the table towards the vicar, "When he's gone you can fire me or do whatever you think fit."

Reverend Matthews sighed, his mind racing, but inevitably he agreed and muttered a reluctant, "Yes."

He owed it to the Bishop to let him spend what might very well be his last Christmas in peace, and besides it was far too late to ask Florence Wheeler to stand in as organist at the service tonight. Yes, minimal disruption, that was what he needed right now until he figured out the best course of action. Archie gave the housekeeper one last glare and returned to his guest in the sitting room.

Bishop Honeywell was fast asleep, a thin trail of saliva trickling from his open mouth onto the chintz cushion under his head and, seeing the old man in such a helpless predicament, Reverend Matthews knew that a few more days wouldn't make much difference. Although he would have to stipulate that Elizabeth kept her chores to a minimum and only looked after the Bishops requirements. Not his, oh no, he wouldn't have a scarlet woman washing his undergarments and ironing his shirts. He shuddered, not really meaning to feel quite so objectionable but nevertheless the sensation was there and he could scarcely believe that Elizabeth was the only woman that he had ever really loved.

Epilogue

Elizabeth Fry peered through the bathroom keyhole watching Reverend Matthews soak himself up to his shoulders in hot bubbly water. She automatically averted her eyes as he climbed out, trying to be discreet but then remembered that nobody could see her and she repositioned her eye. The muscular vicar turned around, slowly drying himself with a warm towel and it was then that she saw the deep scars furrowed along his spine. The housekeeper gasped, her hand clasped tightly over her mouth so as not to let out a sound but she needn't have worried, the clergyman could hear nothing over the gurgling of the water draining out of his bath. Elizabeth waited until the man reached for his robe and then tiptoed silently downstairs.

Archie fumbled with the knot on his dressing-gown and then opened the en-suite door. He was tired, more tired than he ever remembered being before. Catching sight of himself in the vanity mirror he rubbed a hand across his eyes, they were bloodshot and his lids were heavy from lack of sleep. Folding the last of his shirts into the heavy leather trunk, the vicar looked around the room for the rest of his possessions. Not much to show for nearly twelve months in residence he thought, scanning the chest of drawers. His gaze fell upon the photograph at the side of the bed. Two young boys smiled back at him, one just a year younger than the other, both with a mop of blonde hair and both with fire in their souls. He scooped it up and gently packed the silver frame between a couple of sweaters, stroking the glass fondly as he did so.

Bishop Honeywell trembled as he lifted another spoonful of soup to his lips. Most of it spilled down his trousers and he cursed under his breath, wondering where Elizabeth was and why she was taking so long. Eventually she appeared. It had seemed like hours to the old man, but she'd only actually been gone a few minutes. He hoped it was long enough to talk Archie into staying. As the Bishop tilted his head on hearing the house-keeper's footsteps, she slid an arm around his shoulders and shook her head. He grunted, dismayed that she had failed and wondered if she had really tried her best. The spoon clattered down into the porcelain dish and Bishop Honeywell tapped on the tray to get the woman's attention.

"What is it?" Elizabeth whispered, "What's wrong?"

"Mumph," the holy man mumbled, unable to form the words, "Mm, mumph."

Mrs. Fry looked down to the trembling claw-like fingers as they tugged helplessly at a pocket. The bishop managed to nod and sat back exhausted as she reached down and took out the note from inside.

At first it was difficult to make out Bishop Honeywell's ob-scure handwriting, the stroke had taken his once ambidextrous skills and had left him with the ability to write few and ill-constructed letters. Elizabeth took the piece of paper over to the window in the hope of being able to decipher it more quickly.

"Archibald Matthews," she read, glancing over at the sick old man, "Distinguished veteran of World War II, Military Priest, given a full medical discharge in November 1943 due to severe shrapnel wounds sustained on the battlefield. It is noted that Reverend Matthews lost his own brother during this conflict, however it is believed he was able to administer the last rights to Reginald Matthews before he died."

Elizabeth gasped, poor Archie.

Martin Fry sat outside in his Ford Cortina, waiting for the vicar to bring out his luggage. This wasn't how he'd planned to spend New Year but Elizabeth had explained how Reverend Matthews had been unable to accept her past. It didn't bother Martin, he loved her and the past was the past. Funny how some people just couldn't let go of that, he thought, drawing heavily on his cigarette.

Archie heaved his trunk downstairs into the hallway, looking around the vast expanse of the vicarage for one last time. He would certainly miss the congregation, the Bishop, and Elizabeth Fry but nothing would deter him from leaving now, not even his beloved Hector. As if hearing the vicar's thoughts, the huge feline appeared from around a corner, stretching his great body before winding himself around the vicar's legs. Archie ruffled the cat's head and felt a sharp pain in his spine as he bent over.

Nothing had changed. He had come to this place full of nightmares and suffering, both physically and mentally and he would take it all away with him again. The nights of waking up to the sound of gunshots, echoes from a war he had struggled to forget, were as realistic now as they ever were and he still bore the scars to prove it.

Elizabeth ran to the door, realising that this was her last hope to plead with Archie to stay. She couldn't bear the thought of never seeing him again but in a flash the car was gone, heading steadily downhill to the station where Reverend Matthews would disappear to another town and another congregation.

About the Author

Having been brought up in a small village in the English countryside, A.J.Griffiths-Jones has plenty of happy memories from which to source information for her novels. However, it's been a long journey. Spanning three decades and two continents, her career & personal life have taken some incredible turns, finally bringing A.J. back to her roots and a promising writing career.

As a young woman, A.J. left the rolling Shropshire hills behind her & headed to London, where she became fascinated in the world of Victorian crime & in particular the unsolved case of 'Jack the Ripper'. Having read every book available to her on the subject, she started her own mini investigation which eventually led to her first non-fiction publication. However, there was a long period of research necessary before A.J. could finally complete her first book and during the intervening years she relocated to China with her husband and took up a post as Language Training Manager for an International bank. As the need for English grew within the company, A.J's responsibilities expanded until she was liasing between two cities and nearly three thousand employees. An initial two year move soon turned into a decade and the couple found themselves in the vast metropolis of Shanghai for a much longer period than they had firstly intended.

Using their Asian home as a base, A.J. and her better half travelled extensively during their time overseas, visiting New

Zealand, Australia, Philippines, Malaysia, Thailand and many provinces within China itself At weekends they would jump into their Jeep and set off to remote villages and mountains, armed with little more than a compass and a map set in Chinese characters, photographing their trip as they explored. Eventually the desire to move back to the U.K. prevailed and the couple returned to their native land in 2012. It was at this point that A.J. made the decision to fulfill her lifetime ambition of becoming an author.

Initially embarking on penmanship in the historical crime genre, A.J. felt it necessary to create a balance between research and writing. The long hours of studying census reports and old newspapers were beginning to take their toll and, having a natural ability to see the funny side of everything, she decided to turn her hand to writing suspense novels with a comical twist. This newfound combination of writing styles has enabled A.J. to get the best of both worlds. For half of her working week she creates humorous characters in idealic locations, whilst the rest of her hours are devoted to research in the Victorian era.

In her free time, A.J.Griffiths-Jones is a keen gardener, growing her own produce and creating unique recipes which she regularly cooks for friends & family. Her plan is to create healthy, filling meals which will eventually be compiled into a cookbook. In her free time A.J. still enjoys travelling, although these days she spends her time visiting Europe and the British Isles, and takes regular holidays in Turkey where she has a relaxing holiday home, which also serves as a haven to complete the final chapters in her books with a glass of wine and a beautiful sunset.

Another of the author's passion's is reading, especially books that take her out of her comfort zone and into a different historical period.

Nowadays, A.J. lives in a Shropshire market town with her husband and beloved Chinese cat, Humphrey. She regularly gives talks at local venues and has also appeared as a guest speaker at New Scotland Yard, where her investigative research was well-received by the Metropolitan Police Historical Society. The author's professional plan is to write a series of suspense novels as well as non-fiction publications relating to notorious historical figures.

Lightning Source UK Ltd.
Milton Keynes UK
UKHW010415260920
370551UK00009B/483